Orelia Key Bell

Poems of Orelia Key Bell

Orelia Key Bell

Poems of Orelia Key Bell

ISBN/EAN: 9783337408107

Printed in Europe, USA, Canada, Australia, Japan

Cover: Foto ©Andreas Hilbeck / pixelio.de

More available books at **www.hansebooks.com**

POEMS

OF

ORELIA KEY BELL

Αὐτοῦ γαρ εομεν ποιμα.

"For we are his poem."

—Eph. ii. 10.

PHILADELPHIA

THE RODGERS COMPANY

TO THE MEMORY OF MY FATHER,

MARCUS A. BELL,

IN LOVING REVERENCE;

TO

MY MOTHER, MY BROTHERS, MY SISTER;

AND TO MY BELOVED FRIENDS,

MRS. MARCUS W. BECK,

MRS. LIVINGSTON MIMS,

MRS. MARY POPE COOPER,

AND

IDA ASH,

WHOSE AFFECTION AND ENCOURAGEMENT

HAVE BEEN AMONG THE CHIEF SOURCES OF MY INSPIRATION;

TO

MY TEACHERS,

MY PASTORS,

MY EDITORS,

AND

TO ALL WHO LOVE MY SONGS,

IN APPRECIATION OF

THEIR GUIDANCE, THEIR INDULGENCE,

THEIR MANY COURTESIES,

THIS LITTLE VOLUME OF POEMS IS
FAITHFULLY INSCRIBED.

GOD IS LOVE.

1 JOHN iv. 8.

G OD IS LOVE, breathes all nature's minstrelsy,
O n earth, in air, upon the murmuring sea;
D eep-swelling note, it thrills the early dawn,
I nspires the day, and charms eve's dusky lawn;
S oft, sacred lay, it cheers the midnight gloom,
L *ove's voice, e'en heard beyond the silent tomb.*
O sweetest music of the spheres above,
V ast spheres eternal, ever breathing love,
E ternal love, soft breathing, GOD IS LOVE.

M. A. B.

CONTENTS.

LYRICS.

WITH TERPSICHORE.

WITH THALIA.

IN ZION.

IN THE MOUNTAINS OF NORTH GEORGIA.

MELODIES IN MINOR KEY.

SONNETS.

10 CONTENTS.

L'ENVOI.

PRELUDE.

PART I. "REST HERE, LITTLE SONGS."

A home for my poor little pilgrim rhymes.
Nestle ye here with your weary wings.
For many moons, and in many climes,
Ye have journey'd, and brought home precious things:

Gold for bread—ah ! that was sweet—
On bread alone man cannot live,
Yet day by day must we entreat
Our Heavenly Father bread to give ;—

Bright laurel leaves—albeit our brow
Reluctantly to wear them bends ;
And, dearest of all in this life below,
The hearts of a few tried, trusted friends.

And so I have built you a beautiful nest
Of the trees Father planted around the old home,
With a cedar foundation, and bright silver dome,
And wall'd it with pictures of those I love best.

Here are Father and Mother and fair Sister Ada,
And Brother Piromis (we pet-nam'd him Pie—
Which teased him, but he couldn't help it, poor boy !)
And Robert the Papa, and sweet little Cade, O !

And "Grandmother Dearest," my best-beloved friend,
Who gave me the locket to wear o'er my heart,
And the Bible to bond us when we are apart—
And I know she'll be faithful to me e'en to the end.

And "Popie" the precious, and gold-hearted "Creagh,"
Cousin Tishia, who makes the poetical soups,

13

And, to fill out this loveliest of family groups,
Frances, Mary, and Creagh Bell, darling girl-trio.

My Lady of ladies (full-length, hands and all—
The songs tell about her). And, under this latch,
My "Century lovers" (they said 'twas our match,
And upon us their blessings unceasingly fall).

I thought 'twas too sweet when he sent her "*APART*"
(With a bunch of white violets pinn'd on it) out West.
And I doubt not she sat with it press'd to her heart
For an hour or more. Love like this must be blest.

And I doubt not that one of her beautiful long locks
She clipt for him then. (This is *under the rose*,
Little Songs—this is something to hold very close—
One talks very freely 'way down in one's song-box.)

Sweet Anne (we married her too—she who fell
From the moon to get wed.)* And sad-eyed Mary Rex,
Who sings by the sea. My biographers six:
Belle, Annie and Mary, Maude, Mildred and Mel.†

Next comes my good Doctor, from whose laboratory
I get iron tonic and nice pepsin pills,—
Who recommends "changes" and trips to "Tocco-ie,"
And is so kind and modest in making out bills.

Sweet Etta, the wife, with the deep mother-heart—
As she loves "Baby Mary" so do I love my pets,—
And like a rare jewel this little maid sits
In the depths of my Cabinet—a triumph of Art.

See her pure little face peeping up from the box
Into Grandmother's eyes, which look down from the cover,
While the silver and gold of their intertwined locks
Wind all 'round my heartstrings, for I am their lover

*See "*The Lady in the Moon*," page 94.
† Belle K. Abbott, Annie Logan Anderson, Maude Andrews,
Mary F. Bryan, Mildred Rutherford, and Mel R. Colquitt.

"Aunt Lila" and "Annie and Tom" do but seem
  A part of themselves, so to have them is right;
  And dear blind "Aunt Lizzie," with such inner light
  Of spirit to guide her—and blessed "Aunt Em."

Ah! my two charming Sarahs—how differently charming!—
  One chants her *Te Deum* and rolls out her dough
  To perfection! The other just rivets you thro'
  With her jewel-bright eyes—but with no aim at harming.

Mrs. Orme, with the face like a vision of rest—
  A Florida lake 'neath an October moon—
  Whose mission in life is to bring heaven down
  To her circle. One Lily blooms out of her breast.

Here are Corinne the gifted, our Cushman of Art,
  And Emma the genius, and Emma the beauty,
  And Emma the saucebox, the mix'd tuttifrutti
  Of sugars and spices, by turns sweet and tart.

And Helen the nightingale, Ella the queenly,
  Anita the skylark—and last, but not least,
  Leonora the learned, who descants serenely
  In Sanscrit and Browning, our classic high-priest.*

Now my far-famous teachers. Miss Laura the pious.
  The *ponsassinorum* she led us athwart,
  And with French Verbs and Logarithms did edify us.
  But now the poor heathen claims most of her heart.

And those two noble Mallons (sweet be their repose!)
  He doubled our joys and divided our woes;
  She the "Young Lochinvar" taught us how to recite
  The "Bells," and the "Curfew Shall *Not* Ring To-night."

(I was charm'd when she told me "Blind Tom" in the circus-
        scene
  Where the lady, you know, is wound up in the moccasin—
  Quite gave her the creeps. So the music did me.)
  An artist must be realistic, you see.

*Corinne Ruth Stocker, Emma Hahr-Dobbs, Emma Mims
Thompson, Emma Muse-Warren, Helen Knight, Ella M. Powell,
Anita Henderson-McDaniel, and Leonora Josephine Beck.

Aye! I love that kind snake, and I always shall pet it,
For it fetcht me the loveliest tortoise-shell pair
Of opera lorgnettes, that made one see clear
To the end of the world—I can never forget it!

And prithee why not?—if the woman must tread
(So the edict went forth) on the old serpent's head,
Why should not this pet snake fetch from Blind Tom to me
A pair of good lenses thro' which I could see?

The "*Love Hymn*" bewitched her. Not one line drawn thro' it
As she blue-mark'd it 'round in the " Exercise Book "—
And I *think* (I was blushing too madly to look)
That she must have prefix'd the *one-hundred-mark* to it!

But ah! when that "Love Hymn" fetcht me the sweet bonnet—
'Twas the crowning encomium—" a raging success !",
Miss Holroyd had fix'd it. Now let time pass on it
What verdict it would !—(But I seem to digress.)

Here is earnest Miss Millie, who gave candy mice
When we work'd out our Algebra all by ourselves.
And now her great text-books fill national shelves.
Her AMERICAN AUTHORS is call'd *very* nice.

Now my Editors grand—men of cheques and few words—
Gilder, Dana, and Baker ; and shrewd little Clark
(Who pays me for poems, but says, "*Keep it dark !—
Because in the south are so many song birds.*")

Henry Grady, the genius, who "brought us to light,"
And order'd one sonnet a week by the year ;
And the kind *Free Press* man, whose head is so queer
He couldn't grasp anthems—" preferr'd something light."

(By coquettish "*Jaunette*" was his heart quite capsiz'd,
When I wrote an inquiry about her *debut*,
He replied, the engraver was struck paralyz'd
By her charms, and entreated a week more or two.

Ah! but when those brave little vignettes came to light, he
Redeem'd himself wholly : that Night-blooming Cereus
Had something about it so deep and mysterious,
And that rose—'twould have serv'd to adorn Aphrodite !)

Here is dear Mr. Gilder, who liked my "*To Youth*"—
"An exquisite thing—might the Century use it?"
The cheque was ten dollars—how could one refuse it?
Thought I, Here's a gentleman now, in good sooth!

But when for my Christmas iambs* he sent *thirty*,
Why, I fear'd he'd gone mad—should I send back the cheque?
Such recklessness sure the sweet Century would wreck,
Thought I—either that, or I must be a Goethe!

There was one little thing my beatitude checkt tho',
And kept me still humble on *terra firma* —
'Tis my single offense, but it made the muse murmur
And hang a sad head—it was writ in dialect, oo!

Should I keep the vile cheque, in that time of adversity?
I ask'd Mother first. She said, "Don't let it loose."
Then I ask'd my sweet Lady: "Yes, you little goose!
And buy you some ribbons. It shows your diversity."

So I kept the big cheque, tho' my conscience did chide me,
But somehow those coins would not ring in my pocket,
And I can't put that dialect pome in a booklet.
"Thimtimes" I had no dear Grandma to guide me.

Page Baker, my friend of the lyrical bias,
Affects serenades—just died o'er my "*Persian*"—
Toward which Mr. Dana had such an aversion
He return'd it, with words which were other than pious.

"High time that you poets were letting," he wrote,
"The poor bulbul alone." Without pausing to shed
A tear, I hurl'd back at his silver old head
My "*Gathering Roses*"—which went down his throat—

Striking fire from the flint of his benedict heart.
"Bewitching!" he answered—the cheque was a V—
"Sing again for *The Sun*; and accept thou from me
The enclosed *honorarium*." Which so eas'd my smart,

* "*Christmas Thimtimes*."

2

That, in the *Criterion's* earnest behalf,
I ask'd him to sing *us* a song.   Never tarried
His answer—it made us half weep and half laugh—
'Twas simply : "*I use'd to sing songs, but I married.*"

Now this very same " *Gathering Roses* " he lov'd so
Mr. Baker had lately return'd in a huff.
" Just so ! "   I reflected, " here's pointer enough :
They are built *vice versa.*"   And always it prov'd so.

Once Mrs. Frank Leslie wrote such a kind letter—
Which for " *The Dead Worker* " a cheque did enclose,
And ask'd me for tales.   I replied, I knew better—
" The greatest antithesis to poetry is prose." *

And Lollie Belle Wylie, that newspaper artist,
Did so kindly usher some debutante lyrics
Into " Society," along with the smartest !—
Pink-frockt, and bejewel'd with pure panegyrics.

See my faithful song-guardians, Frank L. and Thad E.,
Who rescued my manuscripts from the bad imps,
And managed to give my glad proof-eye a glimpse,
And got editorial setting for me !

" Uncle Remus," whose spring editorials are sweeter
Than half the spring poems that lean upon metre,
Who, altho' a shirker of anapests, O !
Did write such sweet things of my little *Po' Jo'*.

Aye, my little *Po' Jo'* did so work on his graces,
He ardently proffer'd me one of his locks
Of hair to enliven my precious song-box,
But little Clark said it would set it in blazes !

Mr. John Temple Graves so o'errated our fame,
And so shock'd Mrs. Browning's (in the old *Tribune* days ;
For I love my songs " purely, as men turn from praise ")
That we can't face him here, tho' we'll mention his name.

Ah ! that old Southern gentleman, General Walker—
" That modern Sir Galahad," that round-table talker,—

* Wordsworth.

And unlike my "*Sensitive Visitor*" (alack!)
This gallant horseman is sure to *drive back*.

They marvelled why over my maiden bed
The scarr'd face of Angelo hung evermore,
With its sorrow-sunk eyes bending searchingly o'er.
"Lest I grow too happy in singing," I said.

Like guardsmen they stand, those two eyes calling *Halt!*
When the feet of my song touch the quicksands of pleasure.
And the Major, my friend, fills this masculine measure.
Every song-box, I ween, needs a good pinch of salt.

Brave Elizabeth Bisland, whose wee Southern boot
Chased her pen 'round the globe in a dizzy pursuit,—
But Hypomene's love-apple dropp'd on her track
Atalanta hath lured to Arcadia back.

And our kind Mrs. Bryan, whom we spared to the north,
With her tenderest of hearts and her quickest of quills,—
But her term has expired now, and back to her hearth
We have called her to rest 'midst her native red hills.

And brilliant Maude Andrews, whose poems and prose,
As luminous and warm as the sunlight that glows
In her hair and her eyes, cheer our hearths till her "other
Self"* is quite lost in her true self, poet-mother.

And sad-soul'd Mel Colquitt, who dives to the deeps
Of life's troubled waters and brings us up pearls
As lucid and pure as the dewdrop that seeps
To its heart when the Night-blooming Cereus unfurls.

Our Georgia crown-jewel, immortal Lanier,
Melodious Stanton, and that rainbow-woman—
That beautiful, passionate, palpitant human—
Too poised for a meteor, too warm for a star,

Too bold for a flower—rare Amelie Rives!
And that daughter of Pan, who seems to flee from us
More fast than we follow—white-wing'd Edith Thomas,
And behind her a white trail of chastity leaves.

* Referring to her beautiful poem, "*My Two Selves.*"

And gentle Charles Hubner, belovëd of Hayne,
Who laid the last wreath on the laureate's brow,
Aud caught the last strains from his harpstrings, which now
He sends thro' the South iu a soothing refrain.

And Dumas the gifted—that offshoot of Poe,
Whose "*Mockingbird*" echoes the "*Raven's*" own woe,
Aud whose "*Dinner Horn*" sounds from our hill-tops.—And ah!
Here's to grey-hair'd Judge Bleckley, our poet-at-law.

(I can never be thankful enough to the Judge
For carrying my love-lyrics in his coat-pockets.
Most judges, kept busy digesting their dockets,
Or docketing their digests, would call suchlike *fudge.*

My little " *My Love for You is Like a Candle
Burning* " leapt upward and gave such a sputter,
When it heard he had sent it away in a letter,
That the stick danced aud all but run off with the handle !)

Ah, "*Leigh Hunt, my Bird* "—my little song-master !
Who sits in his swing by my desk all the day,
And trills out melodious roundelays faster
Than fancy can follow or passion keep sway.

(He was so precious proud when he sang his way in
That Eden of songbirds, the *Century Magazine,*
He must needs be photo'd !—but it tried the poor lens, he
So friskt his head side to side in his sweet phrenzy!)

Sweet Shelley, the Sensitive ; Keats, his twin-spirit
(If Leigh Hunt, my bird, they might only have known !)—
And that Portuguese lover—my idol, my own—
That best part of Browning, Elizabeth Barrett.

Beloved Longfellow ! what song-box could spare
This face of the singer of life's sweetest psalm !
So benignant, so true.—'Twere as if the pet lamb
Had estrayed from the fold—'twere the one vacant chair.

And here is my Tennysou—my Father's last gift
(On my birthday) before he was laid to his rest—

Thro' the skies of our grief he made many a rift—
Next my Milton and Shakespeare, I love him the best.

Like these *oaks* that he loved he was sturdy and brave,
My Father—he fought with his arm and his pen,
And he died for his loved ones—this gentlest of men—
And now the wild heartsease blows over his grave.

When good old Zaccheus, his Master to see,
The *sycamore* climbed, he left his foot-prints
On the bark, which has crinkled and curled ever since,
So I thought, and I named it my Testament Tree.

Whoever had dream'd that the showy *dogwood*
Would reveal such an exquisite grain at its heart—
Just as some rustic folks, who are clever and good,
Take on a fine polish that baffles town art.

Ah ! the *silver-leaved poplar*—my rainy day tree,
I called it, because in my times of repining,
It always kept turning its bright side to me,
Like Longfellow's cloud with its silvery lining.

The *crabapple* tree always filled me with laughter,—
Such bitter fruition from promise so sweet !
Two-facëd, like some pretty people you meet—
Their smile is *so* sweet, you forgive the bite after.

But, alas, the *wild cherry*—distillery whence
Flowed the red current of innocent wine.
Neither *antis* nor *prohis*, in days of lang syne,
It was patronized freely by us on the fence.

Ah ! I mused as I paused there solemnly,
And gazed on the ghost so gray and stark,
And drew out my blade from the sapless bark,
So all earthly pleasures must crumble to clay.

And the great spreading *fig*—was it too a wraith?—
It had seven branches ; we thought each a heaven,
And we swung there in bliss all the morning and even—
Till a great horned devil-horse upset our faith !

Mighty meetings were held in that noble old tree.
There the neighborhood youth met in grand federation—
Unsectarian we were—every creed, every nation—
Jew, Gentile and African, fearless and free.

Lackaday ! she was dead.   But a lively offshoot—
A grandchild perhaps of the third generation,
Did modestly reach me a handful of fruit—
Which set memory moving in dear palpitation.

And what did I do in return for her grace?
Why, I eagerly basketed all of her fruit,
Then quietly sliced off a piece of her face
To go in my song-box.   She smiled and was mute.

Perhaps she was glad, in her inmost sap,
To be polished, and baited herself for the trap.
Poor figtree ! since blighted by Truth, her remorse
Has refined her somewhat, tho' her grain is still coarse.

As I stood by the gate, in the old back yard,
I saw the veritable nut-dented stone
We had used to crack walnuts and "*scaley barks*" on—
And the struggle to keep back the tears was hard.

All around the green globe has the glory gone forth
Of our grand Georgia *pines*.   Both Hayne and Lanier
Have sung them immortal.   This little splint here,
Is more unto me than a forestful worth.

It was pick'd from the old-fashion'd kitchen door-sill
Where sat Mammy Aggy, once, kneading her bread,
With a snowy bandanna pinn'd over her head—
Poor faithful old soul, I can see her there still.

It was she who when war raised its horrid alarms
Refugeed thro' the flames that leapt 'round the door,
Wrapp'd me safe from all harm in her honest black arms,
And cradled me there till the struggle was o'er.

Here are chips fifty-seven of rare vines and trees
By Major Mims planted 'round lovely " Heartsease."
Tea Olive and *Cypress, Magnolia, Pecan,*
And imported *Evergreens* Australian.

Rubber Tree, Iron Tree, Jasmine, Sweet Bay,
Water Oak, Gold Tree, the *"White Funeral Tree,"*
Wild Peach, and *Honeysuckle, Boxwood, Althea,*
(These grains do but give one a polish'd idea.)

Here the *Delaware* crosses the grape *Scuppernong;*
There the regal *Wisteria* lends a wee prong;
And behold here a glimpse of that rare *Mareschal Neil*
That into my lady's south casement doth steal.

Nor did we forget that superb *Trumpet Flower*
That flags royal welcome in entering this bower.
Dear "Heartsease!" beneath the cool shade of your trees
How many a heartache hath found its surcease.

Behold the *Times-Democrat, Sun,* and *Free Press*
Of one accord meet and each other caress;
And *mirabile dictu !* the *Constitution* and *Journal*
Inlaid side by side in sweet concord eternal.

A slice from Thad Horton's big chair editorial,
Baker's pen, Howell's pencil, cut smoothly in half;
And here Mr. Gilder's sweet Century memorial
Is mosaic'd in, with his rare autograph.

Ah! that darling wee "corner" that fetches us food—
To omit it were basest of ingratitude;
So some strips from this dear *petite mignon* I took
To corner my song-box with, just for good luck.

Rest here, little songs! in your beautiful nest;
It was you brought the straws, and I wove them with love!
And never again from my side shall you rove,
For the mother-love always is surest and best.

Rest here, little songs, 'neath your gold-broider'd covers,
With sweet rainbow ribbons tied true lover-wise,
While jealously o'er you the mother-pride hovers,
And where no hawk-like critic can level his eyes.

Rest here, little songs! Your sweet images roaming
May lodge now and then in the heart of a friend,
(Please God!) but no more from my casement I'll bend
In night-watches to list for your precious home-coming.

Rest here, little songs! It was Heaven who gave
You to me, and I'll live with you close to my heart,
And never again with my own shall I part,
Until the wild heartsease blows over my grave.

PART II. "ALAS, LITTLE SONGS."

Alas! little songs—there's no rest for the just.
My friends cried, "A book!"—in my love and my pity
I arose in the nighttime and—*turned you to dust.*
Alas! "we have here no continuing city."

In the urn of your ashes I mingled the brine
Of my grief with the oil of my sacrifice,
And I watched the sweet incense to Heaven arise,
And I thought that my darlings were saved by that sign.

Saved, from the hot caldron of syndicate steel,
The merciless hammer, the file and the wheel;
Saved from the great Press-Fiend's insatiate maw;
Saved from that vain battle for copyright law.

Saved from pirates. Imagine my lambkins, "Po' Jo'"
And "Jimson Weed" deckt out in cheap paper-frocks!
Nay! better these ashes in this precious box,
Than the dust of the ages—and spiderwebs, O!

Still my friends cried, "A book!" Still I shook a sad head—
And grieved for my little ones—made a low moan
In the night, as the wine-press I trod all alone.
My children were buried—*but they were not dead.*

They came back to me as I toss'd on my pillow.
By the waters of Babylon when I sat down,
Their little hands run o'er my harp in the willow—
They haunted me everywhere!—joy had flown.

How I miss'd their dear lispings, their sweet cunning airs,
Their cute teasing ways when they clamber'd for rhymes,
Their little heartaches, and their clear laughter chimes—
But I miss'd them most nestling about me at prayers.

Their very false steps were now precious to me—
For at times they seem'd bold and their wings must be clipt,
Or out of my power complete they had slipt—
But always they ventured in innocency.

In gentlest obedience, for the most part,
They bent to my wish—and their sweet modest air
As they went on their way, was remarked everywhere.
If I had them back now they might trample my heart!

My obedient *anapests*, pretty and plump,
Always went to their work with a hop, skip and jump.
When I asked them to sing for me, each little miss
Would fall quick into line, with a measure like this.

My twin *spondees* sat so erect,
In church, and looked so orthodox,
The pastor bless'd them on their locks,
And said they must be of th' elect.

And sometimes (I hold it a capital idea)
My best little *dactyls* I took to the play.
With *Blind Tom* my pets were quite carried away,
And they went into lyrics o'er Mad'moiselle Rhéa.

(She *asked* them so archly, what else could they do?)
And " sweet Katie Putnam " inspired them too.
And Corinne's *Po' Jo'* quite bewitch'd them. But ah!
Their little feet leapt when they heard Emma Hahr.

My gentle *Iambs!* ever ready
To guide your brother's foot from stumbling,
How oft you held the sonnet steady,
And kept hexameters from tumbling.

Sadly sometimes would I wander by the melancholy shore,
There to "scan" my pensive *trochees* to the plashing of
    the oar,
Or to teach them from shell-music how to pitch a minor key,
Or to borrow elegiacs from the sea-wind's revery.

But now, older grown, some must needs earn their salt,
And go out to war in the magazine marts—

Perchance to return to me empty or halt—
Aye me ! 'tis the proof-sheet that tries mother-hearts.

But their little home missions return'd them to me,
If not rich, at least honored, and pure from world-stain,
And I gathered them 'round the dear hearthstone again
To share my sweet cup of retiracy.

"*A book*," said my friends, and in accents so bold
That I turn'd very white, and I turn'd very chilly.
Must the critics come down, like the Syrians of old,
Must the critics swoop down, "like a wolf on the fold,"
And gobble my little ones, willy or nilly !

Nay, better cremation—a pure holocaust,
With sighing for frankincense, weeping for myrrh,
While witnessing angels their wings over-stir.—
So the ashes were urn'd—and my darlings were lost.

Now swift-wing'd Repentance beside me awaits.
I weep, like the Peri at Paradise-Gates.
She points to the walls of my conscience, with "Look!"
In God's own handwriting I read there, "*A book*."

Then fall I to my knees and make I a low moan,
And cry I, "Would to God I had died for my own !"
But our Father knows best how to answer our prayer.
When I wake, lo ! the Angel of Memory is there.

She wipes the last tear from my grief-dazèd eyes,
And points a rainbow in my storm-shaken skies,
And leads me, so gently, thro' twilights and dreams
Past the borders of Lethe to Helicon streams.

Over lyrical meadows she measures my feet
Where they first learned to trip ('tis a harder task now),
And in bucolic harness she makes me to plow
Old fields where Pegasus once flew, lightning-fleet.

With yardstick and tapeline the square she makes plain
Where the sonnet, if classical, needs must dovetail
Its *sextette* into its *double quatrain*
(To miss by a hair were ignobly to fail).

Oft she held the candle while I swept the floor
For the tenth piece of silver, and when its true ring
She heard, the nine others she quickly would bring
And help me rejoice while I counted them o'er.

Thus we marshall'd them home, foot by foot, line by line,
Oft journeying at night thro' the storm and the cold
To bring back the lost hundredth rhyme to the fold,
More precious than all of the ninety-and-nine.

Some few still elude me. Perhaps it is well—
Peradventure I leaned on them more than was wise;
Or perchance one day yet, out of uninvoked skies
They will come flutt'ring down in some soft twilight spell.

PART III.—" FAREWELL, LITTLE SONGS."

Farewell, little songs ! Tho' you leave me behind
Sorrowful, lonely, at least for a time,
There is comfort in this, that no motive unkind
Has inspired you with thoughts I would ever unrhyme.

Farewell, little songs ! Sprinkle dews from your wings.
If for life's deeper griefs you have no antidotes,
You at least may breathe balm on its workaday stings
And chase with your music its discordant notes.

Farewell, little songs ! Be not over-ambitious,
Lest, suddenly soaring, you reel down the air.
(Remember poor Wolsey !) The earth is still precious.
Seek, too, the low valleys and spread solace there.

Now if Grandmother Dearest her white hands will spread
O'er my darlings, and pour from her heart's golden vial
A prayer and a blessing, no fate will they dread,
As they go forth rejoicing to meet every trial.

LYRICS.

LYRICS.

TO YOUTH.

TOUCH love with prayer;
    It is a holy thing.
    No dove with snowier wing
Fann'd Eden air.

To mortal care
    Heaven's whitest angel, Truth,
    Entrusted it. O Youth!
Touch love with prayer.

GATHERING ROSES.

O THE deliciousness
    Of the fresh season!
Red roses, white roses,
    Roses past reason!
Out of my gardenful,
    Sweetheart! the sweetest cull,
    Sweetest for posies—
All are so beautiful—
    Which shall my sweetheart cull,
    Sweetest for posies?—
O the unspeakable,
    Untold deliciousness,
        Gathering roses!

Frail, odoriferous
  Sweet-briar'd Eglantere ;
Thorn-studded, cluster-leav'd,
  Pink Ottar roses—
Nay ! Sweetheart, have a care !
Touch not that Circean snare,
Cull not that rose for me—
She will be pricking thee,
  Making my posies.
All are so beautiful,—
  Which shall my sweetheart cull,
    Sweetest for posies ?—
O the untunable,
  Unsung deliciousness,
        Gathering roses !

Gold-hearted, plush-petal'd
  Mareschal Niel roses—
Almost upon your stem
  The scissors she closes ;
Moon-color'd, moss-crested
  Nonpareil roses—
Nay ! thou'rt the day-couch
  Where Luna reposes ;
Virgin-immaculate
  Pale climbing roses—
There Mariposa
  Dreamily dozes.
Passionate deep-center'd
  Jacqueminot roses—
No redder, no rarer
  Blossom uncloses.

All are so beautiful,
  Which shall my sweetheart cull,
    Sweetest for posies?—
O the undreamable,
  Undreamt deliciousness,
        Gathering roses!

Nay! little sweetheart mine,
  Not with the scissors-tips
Cull we the sweetest rose—
  Dear! it blows upon thy lips—
Sweetest rose in Paradise!
Cruellest rose in Paradise!
And this moment, stooping down—
So—I cull it for mine own
(*Spite of thorns within thine eyes*)—
Cull me a whole heartful
  Of life's rarest posies—
O the ineffable
  Eden-deliciousness,
        Gathering roses!

MAID AND MATRON.

THUS a maiden, light and fair,
   To a dame with silver'd hair,
"Tell me how love cometh."

                    "Listen,"
Comes reply, while tear-drops glisten
In the memory-melting eyes.
"You will wake one morn to see
A bluer blue spread o'er the skies
Than was erewhile wont to be,
On the rose a redder red,
A softer down upon the thistle,
And the skylark overhead
Will so soft a matin whistle,
You will wonder why before
You loved not to listen more.
All the earth and all the air
Will seem so fresh, will seem so fair,
You will chide your unbelieving :
'Surely life is worth the living!'
Work for heart and work for hand
Will spread all around you.   And,
Since loving one, and loving much,

Breeds loving many, o'er you such
A sense of charity will steal
That, like Schiller, you will feel
A wish to rush'midst its alarms
And snatch the world up in your arms !
Ah, child ! you will be nearer Heaven
In that hour than it is given
Unto mortals ere to be
Again.''

The maiden, pensively
This time, with hand press'd to her brow :
"Now that you have told me how
Cometh love," she said, "suppose
That you tell me how love goes."
Gravely shook the silver'd head.
"Child, love never went," she said.

PO' JO'.

THRO' mossy glade, by woodland belt,
  Her gentle way she wendeth,
In the calm grace of her dear face
That peace of God all men have felt,
  But no man understandeth.
    Soft ! she hearkeneth (never to me!)—
    Sweetly from topmost bough o' the tree,
    Jo-re-ter, jo-re-ter, jo-re-ter, jo-ree !

O, rare is the scent of the clover bloom,
  The hovering honey-bee sucketh.
The blossom most fair she will braid in her hair,
  Nay! never a bloom she plucketh.
    For the earth and for me careth not she.
     Jo-re-ter, jo-re-ter, jo-re-ter, jo-ree!

All at her feet lieth meadow sweet—
  Surely her eyes she lowereth!—
Only to lift to a gold-blue rift
  Thro' the trees to the sky she adoreth.
    For the earth and for me careth not she.
     Jo-re-ter, jo-re-ter, jo-re-ter, jo-ree!

Now at a turn maidenhair-fern
  Feathereth her pathway quaintly.
Faëries! there hidden to flaunt them when bidden,
  Lie low! for her step is saintly.
    Never her eyes she lets fall from the skies—
    Or only so low as yon heaven-most tree.
     Jo-re-ter, jo-re-ter, jo-re-ter, jo-ree!

The devil's shoe-string doth its bright eyelet-ring
  Slip to entangle her treading;
The broken milkweed poureth out its pale meed—
  All to her foot's unheeding.
    Not even the daisy she noteth—why me?
     Jo-re-ter, jo-re-ter, jo-re-ter, jo-ree!

II.

A RAGGED edge of wheatfield.
　　Capering wheat-bugs, hoppers green,
Rotting logs where lizards play—
That feet so white should stray this way!
　Not a blossom to be seen.
Nay! a ragged yellow weed—
Dog-fennel can it be?
Some poor straggler gone to seed
Or ere it reach'd maturity?
Or faded golden-rod left o'er
From last autumn's treasure-store?—
All amongst the wheat it creepeth,
Scrambleth over rocks and logs,
Out of crevices it peepeth,
In the glazy branch-pool bogs.
Hang-dog head,
Buff-brown eyes,
Shameless stalk, a pole for flies.
Weed unsightliest 'neath the skies!
　　What a dazèd, doggèd air!
　　Desolately, desperately
　　　Reaching, dodging everywhere!
Heaven-set gaze like her's—aye me!
List from out the neighboring tree,
In a plaintive minor key,
　　Jo-re-ter, jo-re-ter, jo-re-ter, jo-ree!

My lady pauseth—bendeth low—
Touch so pure on weed so gross!—
Tenderly, as 'twere a rose,

Plucketh it and saith, " *Po' Jo' !* "—
Plucketh e'en a bunch thereof,
Presseth it, with words of love,
Words of pity and of love,
To her bosom—leaves it there,
Quivering with its tender stir,
As it were a posy rare
Sent by one that loveth her.
Whispereth in rhythm low,
Words of pity and of love,
Bendeth trembling lips above,
Kisseth it, and saith, "*Po' Jo'!*"
While from out the neighboring tree
Comes in shrillest ecstasy,
    Jo-re-ter, jo-re-ter, jo-re-ter, jo-ree!

      Po' Jo'!
Scorn'd by all within thy range.
Ne'er before on thee did dote
Maiden eyes thus lingeringly.
Cattle spurn thee—even the goat
Turns his choiceless nose from thee.
(Greediest weeder of the grange!)
At thee I've heard the farmer swear,
Tangling in his busy share;
Thee the gardener's daughter scold,
Crept into her flower-fold—
Nuisance! everywhere he's found!
Slay him! cumbereth he the ground!
Made to fall beneath the hoe,
And yet—she kisseth him, Po' Jo'!

And who can tell if this Ishmael
Of the woods she so caresseth,
In her heart may not be one warm spot
For me, when mine confesseth—
Slowly homeward wending we?—
　　Jo-re-ter, jo-re-ter, jo-re-ter, jo-ree!

MARIPOSA.

The butterfly is in Spanish " Mariposa." The derivation of
the word is curious, if it may be trusted, and one who has a
right to be heard in the matter (Mahn Elymol. Forschengen,
page 9) advances it with confidence. Nothing in the butterfly
is so striking as the alternations of restlessness when it is on the
wing, and then of perfect quiet when it has lighted. He
divides the word thus, *Mari Posa* or " Sea " and " Rest," first
the restless agitation of the sea, and this presently exchanged
for perfect repose, and finds here a key to the explanation of a
word which has hitherto perplexed all etymologists.—*Trench,
On the Study of Words.*

STILL your winglet, Mariposa !
　　　Flitting, flutt'ring Mariposa !
Some one told me that the first
Butterfly that I saw burst
Out its silky chrysalis
I would have a dress like his.
Still your winglet, that I may
Of your tinsel coat survey
Well the pattern o'er and o'er.
Sure was never seen afore
Such a glorious mantellette !—
All befreakt with gold and jet,
Ruby-red and emerald green,

Amber-ochre, sapphirine,
Satiny and velveteen—
With two ample owlet eyes,
Of that hue that monarchs prize,
A-peering out Minerva-wise.
Why! if I like that were dight
Folks were awe-struck at the sight,
Admiring on what mundane mission
Jove had sent this iris-vision.

Still your winglet, Mariposa!
Gladsome, giddy Mariposa!—
Had not thought you quite so simple!—
There! I've caught you 'neath my wimple.
Now, as low I bend mine ear,
Tell me, Flora's minion, where
All daylong you've been a-flying—
Into what soft secrets prying.
As you woo'd a sip of honey
Of yon blushing-red Peony,
Spied you her forbidden lover
Crouching near her in the clover?
—When you kist the Morning Glory,
Did she tell you her heart-story—
Why it is she dies so soon—
Why can never see the moon?
—Did the violet tell you how
Once she was as white as snow,
Till a ruthless Cupid's dart
Fell and pierced her to the heart,
That the blood did freely pour,

Purpling her forevermore?
Wherefore maidens did, to shame her
Love-in-idleness rename her—
Whence it is, e'en to this day
She doth hang her head alway.

Did pale Hyacinth recite
His sad legend? how he fell
Neath Apollo's fatal quoit—
Whom Apollo lov'd so well!—
That the sweet Laconian youth
All his guileless blood did spill,
Whence to mark Apollo's ruth,
Sprang a waxen snow-white bloom—
Emblem meet for friendship's tomb
—Did Calypso Borealis
Lure you to her iris palace,
Hold you there with honeyed kisses,
As the Ogygian nymph, Ulysses—•
Pledg'd him immortality
If beside her he would stay,
But the Trojan answer'd, Nay!—
Loyal to Penelope,
True to proud Icarius' daughter;
Home-returning then, he caught her
Weaving still Laertes' shroud,
Warding off the amorous crowd.

When the garden-poppy spread
Out for you her plushy bed,
All so crimson, all so cozy,
Can you not to wax so dozy

That you reason'd it were best to
Stop here for a brief siesta ?—
Which e'en until moonrise lasted—
Several golden hours wasted !
Had you been less idiotic
You had shunn'd this snare narcotic.
Did you learn the cause mysterious
Why the sweet Night-blooming Cereus
Shuts her treasure from the light,
Opes it to the thieving night?
—Did the Flaxinella bright
With its *ignis fatuus* lure you—
Only with brown dust to shower you !

Tell me why sweet Eglantere,
With her golden heart laid bare,
And her simple bib-and-tucker,
Shows such temper when you pluck her;
While the city Jacqueminots,
With their frills and furbelows,
And their artificial blushing,
And their hearts all gone to ruching,
Yield smooth arms when lovers woo,
Simply and without ado.

If you keep company with the shoddy,
Haply hoary Polopody,
Darwin's pet, " the old fop fern,"
Smirked you to a waltzing turn.
(Are his jewels really paste ?)
—Ah ! saw you that maiden chaste,
Sad-eyed Anemone, who never,

Since jealous Flora banished Zephyr,
Opes her eyes, except, alas,
To rudely-blasting Boreas?—
Did your wing so gently hover
O'er her, teasing Mariposa,
That she fancied her lost lover
Had come back and did unclose her
Tear-pink eyelids and lay bare
Her conscious heart?—While you, I dare
Say (confess now!), fled to flirt
With Black-eyed Susan malipert—
Or haply down the stream did dart
To take a sail with Floating Heart,
Or walked into the parlor-bower
Or the crafty Spider Flower
(Served you right!), or got your wings
Full of Prickly Cactus stings.

When the Thistledown you blow,
Just so many hairs as cling,
By that number will you know
What the year your fate will bring?

Now, what o' the weather?   Could you tell
From "Shepherd's Weatherglass," Pimper-
Did you count the jewels rare   [nel?
Of turquoise-beaded Juniper?—
Woodbine, Meadowrue and Laurel,
Toadflax, Mayweed and Sheep Sorrel,
Boasting Bladder-Champion—
Tell me something of each one
Cyprus Serge and Rattlebox,

Fever-few and Gill and Phlox,
Yellow Primrose, Daffodowndilly,
Jamestown Weed, and Butterfly Lily,
Devil's Footstool, Cupid's Quiver,
Lady Fingers, Live-for-ever,
Scented Blue-çurls, Bittersweet,
Motherwort and Bouncing Bet,
Beechdrops, Stargrass, Golden Club,
Mouse-ear'd Chickweed, and Sweetshrub
Tansy, Scouring Rush—and O!
I trust you did not slight *Po' Jo'*.

Still your winglet, Mariposa,
Poor imprison'd Mariposa!
What I do is from conviction,
From an artist's sense of duty—
Ah! but you would be a beauty
In my butterfly collection.
Know, I have a gilded frame,
Wherein a hundred of your name
(Mind you! this is just between us)—
Aye, a hundred of your genus,
Are ranged around, as on a rack,
Each with a pin stuck thro' his back
(Tho' that was put there just to keep
Him in his place—he fell asleep
Steep'd in a drop of chloroform—
I could not do him lingering harm).
But not an one in all is there
With you in beauty can compare;
And in the centre will I pin you,

And O! the glory I will win you.
For folks will flock from far and near
To see you, Mariposa dear,
And, seeing you, will ne'er forget
To sing your praise. And yet—and yet—
Somehow I have no heart to-day
To do it. What is fame to thee?
Man alone, with earth-blind eyes,
Fancies, when beyond the skies,
Bliss-embosom'd, angel-crown'd,
Glory's clarion's hollow sound
Can pierce the ethereal vault profound
And into his heart convey
Joyance, e'en thro' Heaven's day.
O mortal thought!—away! away!
Sweet, idle, giddy, happy thing!—
I love thee best upon the wing.
I love thee well, for thou dost bring
Soft thoughts of first-love and of spring.

But mind you, sweet one! do not tell
A single floweret in the dell
About that cruel, gilded frame—
They might not love me quite the same—
They might despise me—and then, O!
Where for a true friend could I go?

Away! away! sweet butterfly!—
What! Mariposa! dost thou lie
So still? The wimple's lifted—see!—
Thou'rt free again. —Ah! could it be
I had my hand too closely press'd—

I thought the wimple let in air.
"*Mari*," "*posa*" "sea" and "rest"—
"*Posa*," "*mari*,"—"posa"——there!

REJECTED.

WARM from the heart, one winter's morn,
    I pour'd a tender-cadenc'd song.
As mothers over their first-born
I doting o'er it hung.

I watch'd each little cunning turn
And thought, "Ah, surely never yet
(So hearts with mother-rapture burn)
Were sweeter verses set."

And with a glowing mother-pride
(Which is not selfishness, because
It loses self in love) I sighed
For all the world's applause.

So one bright morn in early spring
(Green as its grass the memory!)
My little song went journeying
Toward its destiny.

I watch'd each mail with fluttering heart,
And when "Rejected" came in brief,
There mixed with disappointment's smart
A sigh of deep relief.

Thus mother-birds watch fledglings test
Their callow wings, and half in pain,
And half in joy, into the nest
Receive them back again.

Thou wast too weak—thou could'st not soar,
My fledgling ! but to me thou'rt bless'd,
And I but love thee all the more
Because thou can'st not quit the nest.

HEAVEN'S FLOOR.

I CANNOT dream that Heaven's floor
   Is laid with gems or gold,
For one would be to the angel's feet
Too hard and one too cold ;
But O, I fancy that Heaven's floor
Is carpeted with flowers,
More beautiful, if they could be more,
And sweeter than even ours.

The violet I know is there,
In soft profusion sown—
Ah ! it were Heaven enough for me
Were violets there alone,—
The violet to the woodland dear,
The springtime's minion care,
Unchang'd, save as in springtime here
It blooms perennial there.

For I believe that even God
Could not select a hue
More meet to brighten heavenly sod
Than our own violets blue ;
And I believe that even God
A scent could not distill
More meet to sweeten heavenly sod
Than our own violet's smell.

The lilac and the heliotrope,
The pansy and the pink,
And all the beauteous buds that ope
There clusteringly link
About the innumerous golden founts
And heavenly nectar drink
And all the heavenly tapestry
With various patterns prink.

Nay! I cannot dream that Heaven's floor
Is laid with gems or gold,
For one would be to the angel's feet
Too hard, and one too cold;
But O, I fancy that Heaven's floor
Is carpeted with flowers,
More beautiful, if they could be more,
And sweeter than even ours.

AT SUNSET.

IRIS hath emptied
      Her boxful of dyes
Pell-mell into
The Western skies.
Lo! what a passion
Of crimson and blue—
Patches of cameo
Shimmering thro'—
Long cold strata
Of saffron sheen—
Pillows of eiderdown
Bulging between—
Meet for the slumber
Of seraphs, I ween.

Come with me, darling !—
Fling down your book—
Turn to the westward—
Hush, and look !

Which of those tints
Would I choose for a dress ?
Really, 'tis hard
To select, I confess.
You know, like the violets,
I'm partial to blue—
Yes, yes, I would choose
That ineffable hue
The poets call azure—
Come now, wouldn't you ?
I'm sure it was caught
From an angel's eyes
One time as she flutter'd
Down from the skies—
And that red from her lips !—
And that white from her wings !—
And that gold from her crown—
Or her harpsichord strings !—
And O ! that ineffable
Cameo-flush
Was snatch'd from her—
Darling, *do angels blush ?*
But there ! don't answer me—
Look, and hush.

SPRINGSONG.

I LOVE you. I know it
   Because the birds sing
Gladlier this springtime
Than last time o' spring;
The scent of the lilac
That blooms at my door
Is sweeter and subtler
Than ever before.
The breezes are balmier
That come from the dell,
And the grasses are greener
That carpet the fell,
The roses are redder,
The bluebells are bluer,
The white of the lily
More virginly pure,
The pansy more royal,
The jonquil more yellow,
The sunset more gorgeous,
The moonbeam more mellow.
By the green earth around you, the blue skies above
   you,
I love you, I love you, I love you, I love you.

II.

You love me. I know it
Because in your sight
The sun might go out
And I should not lack light,
And e'en if it were to,
Not leaving a spark,

I could feel my way to
Your true heart in the dark.
You love me. I know it
Because in my breast
In your absence there dwells
A delicious unrest—
Which tho' to-day piercing
Exquisitely keen,
I would not exchange
For the crown of a queen,
The bay of a Sappho,
The robe of a Dean—
Nor for all the raised splendors
The oceans between.
By the green world around me, the blue skies above me,
You love me, you love me, you love me, you love me.

LOVE'S FAITH.

IF one should come and tell me that the birds
    Had lost their voices; that the flowers no more
Gave forth soft odors; that for lack of dew
The grass blades droopt at dawntime; that the pearls
Had left the ocean's bed, the sands its shore;
That snow from winter had obtain'd divorce
And lay in summer's passionate embrace;
That frost and fruitage had congenial grown;
That the "Lost Sister" of the Pleiades
Had reappeared in Taurus; that the sun
Had wheel'd his golden chariot to the North—
I might believe him. But if one should come
And tell me you were false—why, I should stand
With folded arms and dart through him a glance

So keenly edg'd with scornful disbelief,
That back he would recoil, like April clouds
Before the advancing sun, and call upon
The mantle of his shame to cover him.

A DAY IN WINTER.

HOW could one live thro' a day like this,
   Sweet! were one not with his books, or in love?
I am both—I am happy—with that dear bliss
Of lovers who have no faith to prove,
Of readers who have no task for heeding,
But read from the sheer sweet love of reading.

The day is dead, and the clouds hang low,
And the winds are weeping a dirge—what tho'?
My life is full—in my heart I know
'Tis only distance keepeth the kiss
         On thy lips from mine,
         On my lips from thine.
No task to heed, no faith to prove,—
Ah! how could one live thro' a day like this,
Sweet! were not one with his books or in love.

APART.

OUT on a leafless prairie, where
   No song of bird makes glad the air,
No hue of flower brings to the eyes
Outward glimpse of Paradise—
A thousand miles and a half away
My Lady is in love to-day.

All thro' her heart are joy-bells ringing,
All thro' her mind sweet fancies swinging,

All thro' her soul are skylarks singing,
For every new southwind is bringing
Tidings glad of her true lover,
And kisses bridge the distance over.
Lips to lips and heart to heart,
A thousand miles and a half apart.

MOONRISE SERENADE.

MOONRISE. And a mellow sheen
All the slumbrous hills is steeping.
Wake, my sweet one, nor be sleeping
Thro' sweet Cynthia's softest phaze—
   Wake and rise and swiftly glide
   To thy lattice, sweet, for O !
   One who wooes thee for his bride
   Sigheth here below.
      I love thee, I love thee,
      My heart, I must confess,
      Can no more love thee more
      Than it can love thee less.

Moonrise. Thro' the casement-blind
Lo, the golden lovelight streaming—
Lady, lady, past my dreaming,
Thou art kind, most kind.
   He who heard thy garment glide
   Swiftly o'er the happy floor,
   He who woo'd thee for his bride
   Sigheth now no more.
      I love thee, I love thee,
      My heart, O happiness !
      Can never love thee more,
      Need never love thee less.

HER WORDS.

IF her silence is golden,
>> What then are her words?
>>> Something purer than gold,
Something sweeter than music of birds
>>> Longtime withholden.

Diamonds? Nay! diamonds are glittering and cold.
Rubies? Nay! rubies are brilliant and bold.
Opals? Nay! opals are fickle, of old.

What then are her words,
>> Since her silence is golden?
>>> Something purer than gold,
Something than diamonds less glitt'ring and cold,
Something than rubies less brilliant and bold,
Than opals, more true—*something not to be told*
>> Are her words.
Something safe down in the heart to enfold—
Something sweeter than music of birds
>>> Longtime withholden.

HER KISSES.

GENTLY as the mists of even
> On the crystal casement settle,
Gently as the dews of heaven
Cluster round the rose's petal,
Softly as the harvest moonbeam
Thro' the midnight stillness slips,
Falls the kiss of her who loves me
On my cheek and on my lips.

Dearer than the blue to heaven,
Than the red unto the rose is,

Dearer than the stars to even,
Than the perfume to the posies,
Precious as the rose to June-time,
As the Sabbath to the week,
Is the kiss of her who loves me
Falling on my lips and cheek.

A MISSION OF CHARITY.

'TWAS at the close of a sultry day
That foretaste of June had brought to May.
With ruthless eye the failing sun
Glanced askance at the havoc he'd done:
For the buff-hearted daisies that sprinkled the field
With joyance that morning had sicken'd and reel'd,
Dazed by the glare of his pitiless glance,
And the leaves on the trees had forgotten to dance,
But hung mouse-still, and gazed below
Where the runlet was almost too lazy to flow.

And a sick girl lay in her dying chair
And prayed for a breath of evening air
To enter her casement and fan her cheek
Where consumption fed with envenom'd beak.
" O, that a breeze would this way wing
And ease to my raging temples bring,"
She sigh'd.
          And away in his western cave
Far, far over the ocean wave,
A soft-voic'd Zephyr, Æölus' child,
Gentle of heart, and brave as mild,
Heard this wail, and he said to himself,
" Now, if a little sylph-like elf
Like me might answer that plaintive cry,

I'd slip thro' a chink, and away I'd fly!—
And why not I?"—as the voice was heard
A second time. So, with never a word,
On a sweet mission of charity bent,
He slipt thro' a chink and away he went!

Now a ship was due o'er the sea that night,
But just ere the harbor loom'd in sight,
The wind at her mast began to fail
And flat and limp hung her every sail,
And the captain on the foredeck trod,
With his hands to his brow and he said, "My God!
Before I can reach her my child will die."
Just then the Zephyr came skimming by—
He heard this wail, in a happy hour,
And swell'd to the utmost in his power.
"What little I can do shall be done,"—
And he lodg'd in the mast, and the ship moved on—
Till safe at last into harbor steer'd—
Then he slipt from the sail and leeward veered.

Now over the fields as he chances to pass
He lightly breathes on the blades of grass—
They nod their heads with conscious thanks
And toss their arms in a thousand pranks.
He lifts the daisies out of their trance
And sprays them with dews till their bright eyes dance.
He sets the leaves on the trees a-quiver,
And hastens the runlet on to the river,—
And all this time he is speeding to where
The sick girl lies in her dying chair.
—Now he enters the casement in time to see
Two strong arms clasp her tenderly—

"My Father! my Father!"   "My darling girl!"
And the Zephyr slips in and lifts a curl,
A golden curl, from a crimson pool,
And he kisses the raging temples cool,
And he slips the soul from the smiling clay
And unto an angel bears it away.

Children, this carries a lesson for you—
See the good even a Zephyr can do.
He went on an humble mission bent,
But on doing good were his thoughts intent.
And see what Providence put in his path:
He reviv'd the daisy with gentle dew-bath,
He gladden'd the leaflet, he dimpled the water,
He claspt to the heart of his dying daughter
A fond old man—and, above all this,
He wafted a soul to the climes of bliss.

BLIND TOM.

I.

HUSH! hearken! 'tis the tinkling of an elfland
    tambourine,
A tintinnabulary sweep of faërie finger-tips.
—Now it soars in silver treble—now it sinks and,
    diving, dips
Down to the very bottom of the deeps of sound,
    I ween.
                Hear it bound and hasten
                Down its diapason,
        Like a mighty current down a deep ravine;
                Upward lightly tripping,
                Now, like children skipping,
        Tripping, skipping, slipping o'er a bowling-green.

'Tis Æolus sighing hither,
Flutt'ring softly as a feather
　From the hovering wing of Nox.
All my senses he entices
With his oriental spices　　　　　[locks.
As his soft mesmeric fingers wandlike overpass my
　Drinking in his breath narcotic,
　Yielding to his touch hypnotic,
I am sinking—I am drifting—I have reached the
Lethe docks.

II.

Was I sleeping?—
Some one weeping
From the cypress hedge is creeping—
'Tis some isolated spirit seeking redress for its wrongs.
　—Nay! some madman—hear the gnashing
　Of his teeth, and see the flashing
Of his eyes!—some madman, certes, who has wrench'd
his prison-thongs.

Hist how his uncanny laughter
Echoes from each startled rafter—
Now, as if possess'd of legions from infernal regions, he
　Shrieking goes around the gable,
　Like the banshee in the fable,
With a wierd reiteration of an eldritch ecstasy.

Was I dreaming?
Moonlight streaming
O'er me sets my opal gleaming—　　[me free—
'Tis some mystic incantation from that spell hath set
　All is calm and still and sober
　As a moonbeam in October—　　　[sea.
As a midnight moonbeam resting on a mid-October

III.

Hurrah! make room for Jumbo!—You gamins! clear
  the track there!
There's a cage of mad hyenas—I say! you'd best
  step back there!
      Tumpty! tumpty, here he comes!—
      Humpty Dumpty, with his thumbs
        Stuck aside his nose.
      —There's a lady on a chariot
      With a snake (how can she carry it!)
      Wound from head to toes.
Whick-whack! goes the whip of the ring-master.
Round, round go the ponies—faster—faster!
      See her whirl!—
      The circus-girl,
    Round and round in giddy gyres.
      Thro' the ring
      Watch her spring!—
A salamander wreathed in fires.
      Now the clown
      Assists her down.
Does he smile, or does he frown?
Hip! hurrah! stand aback!
Humpty's turn now—clear the track!
Whick-whack! goes the whip of the ring-master—
Round, round goes old Humpty—faster—faster—
      See him stumble,
      Watch him tumble!—
In the sawdust roll and fumble!
Now he *faces* his disaster—
      Is he proud, or is he humble?
      Does he grin, or does he grumble?

Hush ! look up, and still your laughter,
Shut your eyes, and hold your breath !—
There's a woman from the rafter
(Samson nerve her !
God preserve her !)
Hanging, dangling by her teeth !

IV.

'Tis a burial in mid-ocean
In midwinter.   With emotion
Round the corpse the crew are crowding,
Round the corpse that they are shrouding
In the snowy winding-sheet.
'Tis the priest that they are shrouding
In the snowy winding-sheet.
This one chants *Ave Marias*,
That one counts her beads by tears,
Some embalm the silver hairs,
Others kneel and kiss the feet.
One—perhaps his mother—tries
To pray aloud—but drops her eyes,
And lifts her empty arms aloft in voiceless agony.
—Hush! O hearken! Do I dream?
Have I cross'd the Jordan stream?
Seraph voices, mingling soft,
Bear my ravished spirit aloft—
Upward, upward to the sky.
I close mine eyes—a sense of Heaven steals o'er me.
Silence profound a moment—then a thunder
Of wild applause.   And lo! that sable wonder,
Blind Tom, the genius, sits and blinks before me.

THE DEAD WORKER.

POOR hands! fold them over her breast—
 So hard, so brown, so cold—
They have done their work and have won their rest,
Tho' they won no gold.
  Theirs was a battle for bread,
  How they struggled and grappled and bled!

Poor hands!—lift them gently, for they
Once lay in a mother's breast,
All dimpled and pink, and cosily
As birds in a nest,
  And a mother's heart once leapt
  As into her bosom they crept.

Poor hands! they have never a ring,
But a mark where a ring has been—
It was all that she had to remind her of spring,
But, to save them from sin,
  She pawn'd it—and so much of gold
  Never again did they hold.

Poor hands! give them flowers to carry
Down into the grave, for they
Were too work-worn and too world-weary
To pause by the way
  And pluck them. Bring lilies and roses
  And fill the stiff fingers with posies.

Poor feet! when the way was high
And stony and nettle-strewn,
We pass'd them by with never a sigh
For the blood-prints under the moon.
  Now that the life-blood is froze,
  Bring the warm gaiters and hose.

Poor eyes! close them to—how they stare!
—Nay! place no gold on that brow—
It was lack of that made the furrows there—
She needs none now.
   She goes to a mansion whose floor
   Is paved with the costliest ore.

Poor eyes! no leisure they had
To gaze up into the sky
And see if 'twas blue, as the poets said—
But now they see;
   To-day they are not so dim
   But that they have open'd on Him.

UNDER VENUS.

UNDER the sun
  There is never a blessing for which I thank
   Heaven
As the power to love you to me has been given—
   Never an one.

Fate may deny me
  The luxury of sailing behind dappled greys
In a plush-cushion'd coach, and in ten thousand ways,
   Fortune may try me.

But who shall dare clip
  The wings of my bliss when I think of the day
My cheek grew as red as a rosebush in May
   'Neath the warmth of your lip.

Gold, gaudy gold!
  If great glistering heaps lay piled at my feet,
I would not loose your warm hand to garner them,
  Sweet!
   —And let it grow cold.

Fame, bubble fame!
   The hill-tops might clarion me unto the skies,
And the skies echo back, and I'd not lift mine eyes—
        But when *you* breathe my name—

Life is too fleet!
   The costliest sceptre that sparkles, mine own,
Could never allure me to rise to its throne
        From mine at your feet.

Distance between us
   May widen with years, but while the blue sky
Arches over us, darling, I'll love you, for I
        Was born under Venus.

LOVE AND FAME.

IF I might focus the combinëd power
   Of all the poets, lens-like, on this hour,
        And pour this page along
        A lofty epic song
That with immortal laurels would mine envied name
    endower,
And 'round me all the garner'd wealth of all the
    nations shower;
And if I might, with like endeavor, sing
A simple love-lay that to thee would bring
        Knowledge of what thou art
        Unto my life and heart,—
Unwavering would I seize the lyre and brush the
    Euterpean string,
And Calliope's trumpet to the four winds would I
    fling.

LOVE HYMN.

SHINE, shine, O Sun! your ample urn
  With all its golden beams o'erturñ,
Till turret-top and tree-top burn
      With amber glory.
Sing, sing, ye birds! with quavering trill
The palpitating ether fill,
Till every quivering leaflet thrill
      With my glad story.
      Yes, tune your merriest roundelay,
      For O! my love will come to-day.

Blow, blow, ye breezes! thro' the dell—
Ye seaside zephyrs! seek the fell
And there my happy secret tell
      To streams and flowers.
Play, play, ye fountains! send on high
Your diamonds till they dint the sky,
And then rebound resiliently
      In rainbow showers.
      Yes, toss on high your diamond-spray,
      For O! my love will come to-day.

Bloom, bloom, ye flowers! my secret dear
Woo from the breezes, then lay bare
Your hearts till all the conscious air
      Is perfume-laden.
Dance, dance, ye brooklets! skip and dance,
Over your pebbles glint and glance—
To see you ne'er again may chance
      So happy a maiden.
      Yes, o'er your pebbles glint and play,
      For O! my love will come to-day.

And ye, O guardian seraphim !
Who listening lean o'er Heaven's rim,
Rejoice ! for even to the brim
    My cup is full.
Thro' Heaven's unbounded latitude
Swell anthems of her gratitude
Who soon will taste beatitude
    Ineffable,
    That saints who pity mortals may
    Rejoice when comes my love to-day.

MY CUP.

WITH the hand I have held to my heartbeat so oft
    To prove that 'twas steady and strong,
She trac'd on a cup, out of tints rich and soft,
    A little bird hopping along,
    The red holly-berries among.

She brimm'd it with love-drops press'd warm from her
    And as a slight memory-boon   [heart,
Bestow'd it upon me,—and now I would part,
    Should angels themselves importune,
    With anything earthly more soon.

It is one of the few things that to me belong;
    That I claim for my own, very own,
And I take out a kiss when I put in a song,
    Lest haply its sweets overrun—
    A new one for every new sun.

Every blossom, I ween, on its nectar hath fed
    In the arms of the breezes that rocks,
From the gay gladiolus of amber-freakt red
    That luxury rear'd in a box
    To the delicate-wove ladysmocks.

Happy emblem of life! may her cup ever be—
    'Tis my wish and my prayer and my trust—
    As graceful, as brimming with sweetness, as
      thee,
    And when be shatter'd it to dust,
    As all things terrestrial must,
May her unfetter'd soul like thy fragrance arise
And float as an incense of prayer to the skies.

TO A WHITE ROSE.

I WOULD the one I love might gaze with me
    Adown into thy bosom's virgin depths,
O pure-white rose! I would that I might place
A loving arm about her yielding waist
And draw her down until her eyes, with mine,
Were on a level with thy modest height,
That she might drink with me thy pureness in,
And feel with me the influence it imparts.

Mute overhead the starry night hangs rapt,
And gloats on thee with all its myriad eyes.
Not even a sylph-like zephyr dares to stir,
Except a-tiptoe and with bated breath,
In tender reverence of thy spotlessness.
The silver-throated warbler of the skies,
Who all day long, to serenade the stars
Behind their sheeny curtains snug-ensconc'd,
Poured forth a tender-cadenc'd roundelay,
Now floods the night with melody, to coax
The moon-queen, on her fortnight's furlough off
Amongst the empyrean wilds, back to her throne,
Amidst the allegianced stars, that she may throw
A silver veil upon thy bride-like brow.

Lo! where the Dian of the marble font
Bends forward to admire thy chastity,
While yonder broad Caladium shields thee from
The pelting of the o'er-fond fountain spray,
    Not twenty paces off,
Thy red, red sister-rose holds social sway.
Belle of the garden, see her nod and smile
And toss the enticing kiss, and woo about
Her feet a coterie of worshippers.
I lay my grateful tribute at her shrine.
God made her, too—she has a heart of gold
Beneath her fashionable plush—her breath
Is fragrant with delicious compliments,
(More oft deserved than else) called flattery
By the less courteous and less beautiful.
She cannot help her beauty—'twas God's gift.
She wins a hundred eyes and hearts; while thou,
O pure-white rose, win'st but one poet's soul.
Yon vestal lily holds herself aloof,
As tho' to say, I'll hold the torch for thee,
But come not near me with thine earthly touch.
Her I admire, too, at a distance. God
Makes every kind of flower to breathe His praise
A different way. But thou, O human-sweet!
O heavenly-pure! thou winnest human souls
To heavenly purposes—not by lofty aims—
By simply being what thou art—thyself.

Let others toil and spin, let others strive—
Thy presence serves; for all who enter there
Are purified, uplifted, and made wise
In thy simplicity. Pure womanhood,
God's last achievement, thou dost typify.

How can I thank thee for this perfect hour!
When thou hast let me look into thine heart
And learn the secret of thine influence.
O that my pen might bless the world therewith,
Even as thou blesseth me, my pure-white Rose.

VIOLET.

MY lady gave me a ribbon red,
   All on a wintry day so bleak.
" Tie it about your throat," she said,
   Knot it close to your pale, wan cheek.
Life is glad, and grieving is sin ;
Earth's happy ones are the ones who win."

And so I carried my ribbon red
   Preciously home to my dear song-bower ;
I knotted it 'round my throat, as she said,
   And there it nestled this very hour,
Close, so close to my pale, wan cheek,
I could all but hear it breathe and speak :
" *Life is glad, and grieving is sin;*
Earth's happy ones are the ones who win."

But there as I sat, there came to me
Out of the past, a memory—
A sad-eyed maiden, tender and true,
With a packet of letters tied all in blue.
I looked on the red, I looked on the blue,
Far better be dead than to be untrue !
" Then choose," said a voice, " the violet,
For here the red and the blue have met."

AN OLD VALENTINE.

WHAT did God make kisses for?
  For the self-same reason
That He made the birds and flowers
  Sing and blow in season.
Kisses, dearest—once again—
Let them sprinkle, let them rain.

Some day, under kinder skies,
  When the mists are risen,
Thou and I in Paradise,
  Walking fields elysian,
Kisses, dearest, like to these,
Ne'er shall cease, ne'er shall cease.

In the happy meanwhile, love,
  Howsoe'er disparted,
Thou and I in time's despite,
  Shall be joyous-hearted.
Kisses, dearest, memory kisses—
This our bliss is, this our bliss is.

"WERE HER KISSES LESS RARE."

WERE her kisses less rare
    Perhaps I would care
  For them less.
Were her hand's tender pressure
A gift at my pleasure,
    'Twere valued at—yes,
  Something less.

There's a rose in my garden smiles all the year thro';
  Its prettiness wearies me soon.

I kiss it—it smiles ; I drop it—it smiles ;
   It smiles whatsoe'er I may do.
   There's another that blushes at every full moon,
         Which somewhat beguiles.
         It teases me, pleases me,
         Never quite scizes me,
           Never quite fills me, as one
         That dropped, angel-wise,
         From unreckoned skies,
         Held me once to its heart—
           And was gone !

THE SONG OF THE STAR JASMINE.

WITHIN the Vale of Circumstance
      Two deadly foes, one dead of night,
Cross'd shadows in the dim starlight,
Cross'd shadows in the dim starlight.
Or was it Providence, or chance ?

" Thy name ! who durst perturb my way,"
   Called one who journey'd toward the stars,
" Keep thee behind thy prison-bars,
   Keep thee behind thy prison-bars !—
   Nor think AMBITION'S flight to stay."

" Cross not my threshold, haughty dame,
   In thy vain journey toward the stars,
   Nor mock my precious prison-bars,
   Nor mock my precious prison-bars,
   HUMILITY my lowly name."

   Or was it Providence or chance ?
   Two deadly foes, one dead of night,

Lay dead beneath the dim starlight,
Lay dead beneath the dim starlight,
Within the vale of circumstance.

And as by way of compromise,
From out the ashes of the two,
Lo I, a pale STAR JASMINE grew,
Who ever hug earth's prison-bars,
Who ever hug earth's prison-bars,
Yet ever strive toward the skies.

THE POET AND THE MOTH.

IN contemplation lost, a poet sits,
  His eye turn'd westward. Thro' the lattice comes
The last faint-lingering breath the gloaming sigh'd
When thro' her parti-tinted veil of sheen
She saw the round-fac'd herald of her doom
Smiling triumphant o'er the opposing hills.
Within the twirling texture of his brain
A wingèd poem lies enmesh'd: he fain
Would, yet would not, cage it for aye in words,
Ere haply it escape and go the way
Æreal it came, unlocalized.—
(For the poet's first impulse is to give
Freely of what to him is freely given) —
And yet 'twas passing sweet to hold it there,
With dews of heaven fresh upon its wings,
A secret visitant.—With sudden turn
He lights the lamp, and o'er the inviting page
Pours out his mood—when lo! a guileless moth,
With tinsel wings, gold-dusted, wilder'd by
The dazzle of the light that lur'd it in,
Falls blinded o'er the moisty page, and leaves

Athwart it, where his winglets trail, a blot
Big and uncouth.　The poet lifts his hand,
Vexation knits his brow—with one true aim
Down comes his ruthless fist.—A tiny heap
Of powder'd tinsel meets his softening eye.
He drops the pen.　The poem has escaped.

AFTER-PEACE.

WHEN he was here a sharp remorse
　　　Shot ofttimes thro' the bosom's core,
But it was still'd forevermore
When thro' the gates they bore his corpse.

His nature, cast in nobler mold
Than ours, and divinelier-strung,
With our ungentleness was stung
When loving blame wax'd overbold

To shapen his unworldliness
Subservient to our worldly ends.
We who were sent to be his friends
Seem'd oftenest to bring distress.

And oft we said, When he is dead,
Remorse, with keenlier-temper'd knife,
Will pierce thro' all our after life
For this thing said, that left unsaid.

But now that death hath brought surcease
Of toil, and rais'd him to his sphere,
We feel he knows we lov'd him here—
He understands—and we're at peace.

SWEET-SHRUBBING.

MY loves and I sweet-shrubbing went
    All on a balmy April day.
Three summers they—and I ?—ah me !
    What recketh time when the heart is gay ?

At first my loves were coy and shy,
    As new-unprisoned birdlings are—
Now leap and fly thro' the under-sky,
    Where every blossom seemeth a star !

Clustering bluets, Pleiades-white,
    Wild strawberry blossoms as yellow as Venus—
And O ! the laughter following after
    We pluck them and share them between us.

O'er dale and dune, right valiantly,
    Thro' many a brambleberry toil,
We wend our way till close of day,
    When lo ! appeareth the purple spoil.

We knew it first by the air around,
    Ere down in the marsh we glimps'd it. See !
A great fresh clump !—and over they jump
    Into the cool green sedge with me.

And never an Israelite brought back
    From the Promised Land his Eshcol wonder
With head more proud than those we bow'd
    That royal weight of sweetshrubs under.

LEX TALIONIS.

ONLY suppose
     I were this rose,
And thou should'st stoop down and kiss me,
     Then pass me by—
     Of course I should die—
And thou?—O thou hardly would'st miss me.

     But when Spring came again
     I'd return with the stain
Of thy lips on my deep-bruisèd petals;
     Should'st thou then stoop to pick me,
     Take care! I would prick thee
Till blood trickled down o'er my nettles.

*   *   *   *   *   *

     Spring comes again.
     I return with the stain
Of thy lips on my deep-bruisèd petals;
     Thou stoopest to pick me
     Once more.   Do I prick thee
Till blood trickles down o'er my nettles?
Nay! I bend like a reed 'neath the old-time caresses—
And burn a live-coal in the black of your tresses.

LOVE.

With apologies to Raphael and Lea, in Moore's "Songs of the Angels."

TWO spots in all the world there are to me:
     The one bright, radiant spot
Where beams her face,
The one broad, dreary space
     Where she is not,
Two spots in all the world there are to me.

GRACE.

I KNOW not what, but when she lifts her hand
  To point a flower's perfection, with " But see !
How exquisite !" the blossom magically
Assumes a rare, new fragrance, as by wand,
And all the quicken'd sense is forthwith fann'd
  With wave on wave of Eden fragrancy.
A subtlety—we may not understand,—
  Past painter's brush, past poet's minstrelsy.

JAUNETTE.

SHY violet, feigning with thy conscious lashes
  To ward aside the enamor'd earth's addresses,
Yet, when the jealous skies, with lightning flashes,
  Would snatch thee home, dost hug it fast—O this is
        Jaunette's own way,
        So timid—yet
        Coquette ! Coquette !

Frail morning glory, who, ere the day dare face the
  Darkness, upliftest honeyed mouth for kisses ;
But when its kindled passion would embrace thee,
  Tuckest thine head and vanishest—O this is
        Jaunette's own way,
        So gracious—yet
        Coquette ! Coquette !

Plain brier rose, who wearest thy bad temper
  Outside thy sleeve, beneath thy scanty tresses
A heart of gold—I dare my touch (*sic semper !*)
Shatter'd thine heart : thy nettles cling—O this is
        Jaunette's own way,
        So candid—yet
        Coquette ! Coquette !

Rare Jacqueminot, whose tapering waist awaitest,
  Thornless and smooth, mine amorous caresses,
Yet when I fain would clasp thee, concentratest
  An hundred briers in one thorn—O this is
          Jaunette's own way,
          So cultured—yet
          Coquette! Coquette!

Sad-eyed Anemone, a pale recluse
  (Since Zeph'rus' fate) for thee no second bliss is;
Yet let wild Boreas once his passion loose,
  Thou blushest forth a twinkling star—O this is
          Jaunette's own way,
          So constant—yet
          Coquette! Coquette!

Night-blooming Cereus, scorning Sol's advances,
  Retired within thy convent's chaste abysses,
Off with thy hood! thou'rt scheming soft romances
  With ieweled Nox at trysting-time—O this is
          Jaunette's own way,
          A saint—and yet
          Coquette! Coquette!

Jaunette! star-princess of the blossoming skies,
  Who guid'st my poor heart out earth's wilder-
      nesses,
Now waxed so dazzling bright, dost blind the eyes
  Erewhile thou woo'dest Edenward—O this is
          A most cruel way,
          Farewell—and yet
          Jaunette! Jaunette!

A MAY REGRET.

I DO repent me of the ungentle things
   I said about thee, Winter. Had I known
That that rime-frosted mantle 'round thee thrown
Hid roots of such luxurious blossomings,
Of royal heartsease, lilies gold-besprent,
And milk-white pinks, for Spring's bewilderment,
I had not slamm'd the door so in thy face
When thou wast fain to be my midnight guest,
But e'en had ask'd thee to the cosiest place
And of kind welcomes given thee the best.

A SPRIG OF PERIWINKLE.

A SPRIG of periwinkle from the grave of Dolly
   Madison.
The prettiest and the wittiest first lady of the land
   she was,
      And like this periwinkle
      Her laughing eyes did twinkle,
But now the periwinkle twinkles all above her
   eyes, alas.
      Sweet Dolly Madison!
      O the hearts and hearts she won!
She was a merry lady tho' the proudest in the land,
   I ween.
      At old Montpelier
      I pause and drop a tear
For the dancing and the laughter down these dim old
   avenues have been.

And yonder looms the Blue Ridge—there the fields
   of old Manassas lie—

The Rapidan trips 'round the hills—so swift her merry
    tripping was—
        Yes, like the periwinkle
        Her dancing feet did twinkle,
But now the periwinkle twinkles all above her
    feet, alas.
        Sweet Dolly Madison!
        O the hearts and hearts she won!
She was a merry lady tho' the proudest in the land,
    I ween.
        At old Montpelier
        I pause and drop a tear
For the dancing and the laughter down these dim old
    avenues have been.

RAIN IN THE DUST.

RICH incense of roses, rare violet breath,
    The subtle aroma of mountain blue-bells,
The sensuous perfume of magnolia bloom,
The Edenic fragrance of white asphodels—
Aye! but give me the odor that rises up just
After showers in summer of rain in the dust.

    Then roses and violets and white asphodels
    Intermix with magnolia and mountain blue-
        bells—
    All odors that charm intermingle and rise
    Till the earth seems a censer that's swung to
        the skies.
Yes, give me the odor that rises up just
After showers in summer of rain in the dust.

"THE ETERNAL HOPE."

STARLESS midnight in December
　Ne'er was blacker, ne'er was colder,
Than his heart, a Dead Sea boulder,
A burn'd out crater, with no ember—
　" Lost, past restitution lost."

Lo, a little child one even
Pass'd his way : her baby prattle
Rous'd dead passions to pitch-battle,
As when Michael's band in Heaven
　Warr'd with the Satanic host.

Never heard I of him after—
If he rose or deeper fell,—
But this lesson learn'd I well,
While the world hears baby laughter
　Souls can never quite be lost.

UNDER OUR FLAG.

Two Pictures.

I.

HALF-couch'd in crimson plush, one slipper'd toe
　Daintily resting on an ottoman
Of oriental dyes, a lace-wrought fan
Concealing half her bosom's jewell'd snow,
She lolls luxuriously ; while, breathing low
A honey'd iteration from false lips,
Over her half-moon'd fingertip he slips
A rich troth-token of transplendent glow.

II.

Down in his cavern home of dawnless night,
Sweating he toileth for the precious stone,
While from his half-fed lips goeth up a moan
For her who sitteth in the dim lamplight
Far up above, and with red aching sight
Weaveth the web-like lace with rare device,
While to her milkless breasts, with plaintive cries,
Cling baby lips all pinch'd and hunger white.

TENNYSON—IN OLD AGE.

(A Reproach.)

BECAUSE our poet-king
        Cannot so grandly sing
As when the noontide ichor coursed along his veins;
        Because his tottering lyre
        Has lost its pristine fire
In that dear after-calm which comes when passion
        wanes;
        Shall we for this, forsooth!
        Proclaim his lays uncouth,
And drag his glittering name the slimy streets along?
        Nay! but with tenderer grace
        Heart-press each waif that strays
From this the precious second childhood of his song.

AMELIE RIVES.

(On Reading Her Early Poems.)

O WHAT so bright a star,
        On what so soft a morn,
Shed influent ray that happy day,
Amelie, thou wast born?

O what so rare a bird,
From what so golden clime,
Hath taught thy throat its silvery note
To lift in liquid rhyme—
Columbia's nightingale of song,
                    Amelie.

From moon to moon we sit
And northward listening lean.
Leap up! rejoice! for hark, *a voice*
Thro' all the rhythmic din,—
A voice from out a soul,
A young voice, thro' a wail
Pulsing its way, more fresh than they
That quicken'd Tempe's vale—
Columbia's nightingale of song,
                    Amelie.

O what so stern a fate,
In what so ungentle wake,
Thy midnight breast hath taught unrest,
Thy guileless heart to break ?
We love thee, dainty soul.
If grief or memory-wraith
In thy fair glade have cast its shade,
God lift it from thy path !
Columbia's nightingale of song,
                    Amelie.

And yet we need thee so,
Even as thou art, to sing,
Upon thine harp we would not warp
One delicate minor string.
Long live to sing and soar !
Yet, in thine higher soarings,

6

For clearer truths than came in youth's
First passionate outpourings,
Thou need'st must reach in vain.
Loving and life are one,
And hearts must bleed while hearts have need
Of love beneath the sun,
Columbia's nightingale of song,
                         Amelie.

CORINNE.

CORINNE!   Corinne!
I thought to catch thine accents in my song.
Alas, they slipp'd and glided 'twixt my rhymes
And trickled in and out among
The syllables of my words.
As easily might I forecast the chimes
That burst from golden-throated mocking-birds
As catch thy gliding cadences within
The meshes of my rhymes,
            Corinne!   Corinne!

And, like that peerless spirit of the wood,
Misnam'd, thou *interpretest*—not echoest back
In soulless iteration.   As I stood
And listened to your plaintive *jo-ree* cry,
That morning in midwinter, thou did'st take
Me back to July forests, where the sky
Kisses and melts into the pines—blue-green
Even as thy genius eyes,
            Corinne!   Corinne!

RHEA.

CHARMANT! I wot not in what witching wise
　Our fond old mother-tongue could perk herself
In Frenchy airs! Plum'd in her pretty pelf
Of smother'd *s*'s, silent *t*'s, soft *i*'s,
In lisping syllables that fall and rise
In unexpected rhythm, like a sylph
She glints across the dusty classic shelf,
In scorn of startled Webster—aye, defies
Her very Pujol! But what tho'? Our heart,
She reaches that, despite! and that is where
Words lodge and live, or glance and stillborn fall.
Rare Rhea! we love thee in thine every *part*,
But in the perfum'd presence of thy fair
Sweet woman-*self* we love thee best of all.

RED, WHITE AND BLUE.

A telegram to little Miss Ruth Cleveland on her arrival in the nation.

BABY white, with starry eyes,
　Take these little stripes of song,
With red kisses strewn along,
From a poet 'neath blue skies.

A SIMPLE NOTE OF THANKS.

A SIMPLE note of thanks—yet 'tis
　Here a queen's heart its grace doth prove—
Columbia's queen, whose coronet is
Columbia's admiring love.

Now on her beauteous brow serene
A brighter gem by hand of God
Is set, that makes her doubly queen—
The jewel of young motherhood.

Out in our nation's firmament
Her memory will shine apart,
Like Wordsworth's star, pre-eminent
For beauty, pureness, grace of heart.

But ah! her delicatest deed
Of grace, that all the rest outranks,
Is, that she took the time to read
My lines, and send this note of thanks.

WHAT FLOWER IS BABY MARY?

WHAT flower is Baby Mary?
   A rose? Ah, no!
That breathes and blows
An hour, then goes
To make its bed beneath the snows.
What flower is Baby Mary?
   A rose? Ah, no!

What flower is Baby Mary?
   A violet? Nay!
That lifts its head,
Then droops it, dead,
And all its joy is spent and sped.
What flower is Baby Mary?
   A violet? Nay.

What flower is Baby Mary?
   A white asphodel,
That oped its eyes 'neath Eden skies
To bloom for aye in Paradise.
This flower is Baby Mary—
   A white asphodel.

BABY'S FIRST JOURNEY.

HOLD out your arms, nurse—
  Steady, my little one !
Let go my fingers, miss—
  You've still got the middle one.

No crawling—learn to walk—
  Don't jump—don't fidget—
Gracefully—head erect—
  Step, little midget !

Don't stare so woe-begone,
  The carpet is downy.
Don't squat as guineas do !
  Don't climb, like Bunny !

Now be a Joan d'Arc !
  Hip ! hip ! one, two, three !
What's that in nurse's hand ?
  Sugar-plum, seems to me !

No need to coo like that,
  Full time you learn, miss.
Only by labor hard
  Good things we earn, miss.

Once more ! and up again !
  Now a step forward !
Don't clutch my girdle so,
  You little coward !

See, nurse, she's made a step
  Into the rosie-red ;
One more will take her clear
  Over the posy-bed.

That's papa's precious girl!
        What a sight he misses!
Nurse, give up the plum, while I
        Smother her with kisses!

"TOGETHER GREW UPON ONE STEM."

(Grandmother—Granddaughter.)

TOGETHER grew upon one stem
        A white rose and a white rosebud.
Gazing, full of love, on them,
Close beside, a poet stood.
        And O! I said, together so
        Might they always bud and blow.

The bud reached up toward the rose,
The rose stooped down toward the bud,
Each leaning on the other close,
Clasping, kissing all they could.
        And O! I said, in wise like this,
        Might they always clasp and kiss.

A playful zephyr slipt between,
Unclaspt their arms in mock disdain,
Then friskt them into friends again
More fast than ever they had been.
        And O! I said, in this coy way,
        Might they always frisk and play.

But Time, who is the rose's friend,
Is, too, the rose's ruthless foe,
And brings, with certain pace, we know,
Alike to age and youth—an end
        Then O! I said, by art's sweet grace,
        I'll set them in the Future's vase.

TO THE AUTUMN WOODS OF EIGHTEEN-EIGHTY-EIGHT.

O AUTUMN Woods of Eighteen-eighty-eight!
  How can you smile and flaunt your yellow arms,
In mockery of danger's flag-alarms
Thick waving o'er our stricken Sister-State.
     Sweet Florida lies dying
      While o'er the hills you're flying,
    A-pleasuring in holiday array!

Twelve moons ago I bounded o'er your hills
Blithe as your swallows and as careless-merry,
I gathered jewels from your whortleberry
And dipped my fingers in your laughing rills.
     To-day I cannot bear
     Your red-and yellow glare,
    But turn mine aching eyes the Boreal way.

Fling down your glittering sceptre, goldenrod!
Take off your royal ensign, purple phlox!
Shake the haw-rubies from your golden locks!
Put on your sackcloth, don your sombre hood!
     And bid your breezes sigh
     A dirge-like melody
    In sympathy with our sweet sister's passion.

Then o'er your darkling hilltops, lightning-fleet,—
Speed with a message to the Ice King's home,
And bid the great Physician this way come,
Arm'd with his sheets of snow, his pills of sleet,
     Fair Florida to save
     From an untimely grave—
    The pet and bridal state of our proud nation.

IN FLORIDA.

WHO'S yon merry maiden,
   Dancing down the dune,
Roseate robes array'd in,
Arms with blossoms laden,
   On her lips a tune,
   In her hair the moon?
Sure yon radiant maiden
   Is the Lady June.

Nay! yon lovely maiden,
   With the step so fairy,
Roseate robes array'd in,
Arms with blossoms laden,
   Tuneful lips and cherry,
   Crescent-crowned and merry—
Nay! yon radiant maiden
   Is young January.

IN AN ORANGE GROVE.

'TIS day—and yet the stars!
   Sure heavenly constellations these!
There's *Venus!* and there's *Mars!*
And yonder faint the *Pleiades!*

The *Sickle's* curve!—and lo!
Orion's ruddy belt is plain.
The *Serpent's* sinuous path—and O!
Behold great " *Charles' Wain.*"

Ofttimes I've prayed the prayer
On earth let Heaven's kingdom be,
But little dream'd I now and here
The beauteous symbol thus to see.

BAY AND PALM.

BEHOLD yon green baytree :
   Close to the ground it flourisheth ;
Emblem of man's mortality,
To it the purer air were death.

Behold again yon palm :
Only in higher air it thriveth;
Emblem of spirit, lofty, calm,
Ever towards the stars it striveth.

"ON POINT OF SPANISH BAYONET."

ON point of " Spanish Bayonet "
   See Mariposa calmly sit—
Which I, with all my wisdom, must
Avoid lest in me it be thrust.
Sweet Edith Thomas would declare
'Tis " frailty's shield " preserves him there.

And yet methinks, sweet butterfly,
Rather than thee I would be I.
Thou thinkest that is Heaven—and yet,
'Tis point of Spanish Bayonet !
Give me the little grain of sense—
Take thou the blissful ignorance.

O LILIES OF ST. JOHN'S.

O LILIES of St. John's ! No schism
   Can ere apostate you to soil
Of earth. Your life, one long baptism,
Exempteth you from mortal toil.

A FLORIDA TWILIGHT.

I SIT beneath a golden-fruited mandarin.
  To westward, thro' the zephyr-swaying emerald
    boughs,
I glimpse the placid bosom of fair " Loch Katrine,"
Beaded with mother-of-pearl.   To eastward, rows
On.rows of topaz oranges, with here and there
A jacinth tangerine, foil'd by a silvering grape,
While conscious twilight spreadeth o'er the whole
    landscape
An amethystine veil looped with one diamond star.

NEW MOON ON ST. JOHN'S.

'TIS new moon on St. John's,
  And a charm is on my soul.
And what care I which way the die
Be cast or the fate-wheels roll?
Can souls in Heaven be conscience-riven
For souls that have miss'd the goal?
'Tis new moon on St. John's,
And a charm is on my soul.

On northward heights they freeze,
In southward swamps they burn,
But God is above and I may not move
The scales of doom to turn.
So what care I which way the die
Be cast, or the fate-wheels roll—
'Tis new moon on St. John's,
And a charm is on my soul.

SWEETHEART JANUARY.

THRUSHES in the liveoaks
  Make my pathway merry,
As I rove to meet my love,
  Sweetheart January!
My new love, my true love,   .
  Sweetheart January!

Au revoir, December dear!
  Poets may not tarry.
She hath violets in her hair,
  Moss-veil'd January!
My fair love, my rare love,
  Sweetheart January!

In her breast are lemonbuds—
  Of their thorns I'm chary—
I would kiss thee an' I dared,
  Blushing January.
My shy love, my coy love,
  Sweetheart January!

In her hands is glittering gold—
  Maid unmercenary!
All thy treasures I would hold,
  Bounteous January!
O sweet love, O fleet love,
  Sweetheart January!

For new charms I'll pass thee by,
  Grown of thine aweary,
But to-day for thee I'd die,
  Darling January!
O glad love, O mad love,
  Sweetheart January.

ON LAKE MINNEHAHA.

LO! I have awaked in Fairie-land,
    Where oranges burst thro' the glittering sand,
And lakes, like diamonds, circle and deck
Fair Florida's beautiful swanlike neck—
In a spot of perennial summertime weather,
Where the gulf and the ocean come nearest together,
I sit 'neath a golden tangerine,
Whose drooping branches serve to screen
The sensitive strings of a Georgia harp
From breezes that worry and beams that warp.

Just down the orange avenue
I glimpse the " laughing waters " blue—
Beautiful Baby Minnehaha,
Nourish'd by Dame Palatlakaha—
She smiles and beckons and dimples with glee
And kisses her jewell'd fingers at me,
And tosses her tresses, and calls, " Come down
For a frolic!"   I answer, "Anon, anon!"

Clustering grapefruit hangs near the door,
Like Eshcol clusters from Canaan's shore,
Borne on a staff—and lo! and behold!
Little Brownies are springing up out of the mold—
Shade of St. Nicholas!   Whence did they come?
There's Alton and Hulsey and Nellie and Tom—
Now they scoot down the sand-slope and into the
        brake—
Now the boys are half-way to their knees in the
        lake—
I scream to them vainly.   Now each little trooper
Wades out, with a mussel to bake for my supper!

Now shadows are falling o'er valley and dune—
Minnehaha is waiting for Grandmother Moon
To kiss her good night—all bedight in a gown
As white as May blossoms and fluffy as down,
Her pretty red cloak and her dainty blue shoes
Laid aside till to-morrow. And now how she coos
And claps and flings kisses, for Grandmother Moon
Is peeping just over the hilltops, and soon
The mists will have vanished and left her round face
All dimples and smiles for the darling embrace.

FAREWELL TO LOCH KATRINE.

THE pines stalactite moss into the wave,
   The wave stalagmites it again to shore:
From where my shallop drifts I seem once more
To dare the dangers of the Luray Cave.

As some dread mystery of the Holy Ghost
Upholds us when the eye of faith we lift,
Thus in my faithful shallop do I drift
Safest and surest where I seem'd most lost.

I turn: a trillion diamonds twinkle out
Across the wave—now into opals melt—
Now fire into an amethystine belt,
Girding the bosom of the lake about.

As Father Son had thought it best to go
From his beloved earth a little while,
But left behind, in one bright after-smile,
The promise of the Comforter. And lo!

Where now she shimmers forth, the Evening Star,
To guide me homeward o'er the darkling lake.
Sweet friends! I'll greet you in morn's earliest wake.
Now God be with you—for in God we are.

THE LADY IN THE MOON.

(Music by EMMA HAHR.)

(ROMANZA.)

'TWAS moonrise at Luray,
    In the heart of the Shenandoah vale;
Sweet Anne raised her eyes my way
And thus my credence did assail:
    " There is never a man in the moon," quoth she,
        But a lady, as plain as a lady can be."
        "Oho!" said I—and the mystery
            Of the moon's soft charm was clear to me.

Sweet Anne left me. We builded a bridge
Of kisses over the stern Blue Ridge.
And every night at moonrise she
Cometh back over that bridge to me,—
        Over the mountain, the vale and the lea,
        This sweet moon-lady that dwells by the sea.

IN THE CAVERNS OF LURAY.

THRO' all those mystic chambers subterrene,
    Uncharm'd I pass'd, till 'neath the " Angel's
        Wing,"
That sentinels the " Grand Cathedral " door,
    I paus'd, and heard the " Organ " play within
    A soft *Te Deum*,—for this seem'd to bring
    Down Heaven where Hell was pictur'd hereto-
        fore.

But in those mystic chambers subterrene
Was something I could better understand—
Something to text a sermon from, I ween :
The " Ballroom " with the " Graveyard " close at hand.

AN UNSUNG SONG.

O FOR the art
    To utter my heart !
In it now flutter thoughts sweeter, I ween,
Than ever entangled in rhythm were seen,
Which into expression no coaxing will start.

    Sentiments sweeter,
    Purer, completer,
Than ever gusht forth from the Helicon bard
In melody dulcet ; yet—O, it is hard !
Persistent they shun all acquaintance with metre.

    Rhyme they'll none of it—
    Think they're above it,
Haply—woe's me ! how the strong guiding hand
That turn'd glowing thoughts into shape at command
Of the Mantuan Master this moment I covet.

    But never a letter
    Shall hold you in fetter,
Sweet sentiments born in my bosom to-night
Unutterable.   Well, peradventure 'tis right.
At least for your presence I feel I'm the better.

MY DREAM.

I LOVE you, I love you.   They call you my dream ;
    And you are ; I know it by one true test :
Toil how I may thro' the long happy day,
My dreaming hours are my best.

My Dream ! O my Dream, my beautiful Dream !
My dream of heaven-on-earth come true !
They can no more keep you out of my sleep
Than they keep out of roses the dew ;

They can no more bar you out of my prayer
Than they bar out of heaven the blue.

My Dream—yes, my Dream—my one true Dream,
That out of sleep's valley dawn'd none too soon;
They can no more shut you out of my hope
Than they shut out the roses from June;
They can no more bar you out of my life
Than they bar the tides from the moon!

My day-dream, my night-dream, my dream-within-
    dreams,
The one dream of warning I watch for and heed.
And my one wish supreme, my beautiful Dream,
Is to live my way up to thy need—
By silence, by song, be the way short or long,
By patience, by prayer—whatever the stair,
To climb my way up to thy need.

"MY LOVE FOR YOU IS LIKE A CANDLE BURNING."

MY love for you is like a candle burning
    In a dark room—your all that shows the way;
Emerg'd now in the light of entering day,
'Tis set aside to await the night's returning.

My love for you is like a star in heaven,—
    Day dawns, 'tis needed not and seems to die;
    And yet it waits there calmly in the sky
To guide you homeward thro' the darkling even.

Thus would I have my love for you remain.
    'Tis friendship's better part. The whole world may
    Rejoice with you when all is glad and gay,
But let me be your balm in hour of pain.

LILIES FOR THE BABY'S GRAVE.

AS a pearl tost by the wave,
    As a star that melts in day,
So the baby pass'd away.
Lilies for the baby's grave.

As a pearl tost by the wave
From the world's great shore of doubt,
So the little life tost out.
Lilies for the baby's grave.

As a star that melts in day
Seems to lose the light it gave,
So the baby pass'd away.
Lilies for the baby's grave.

WELCOME, BABY MARGARET.

MARGARET: "A PEARL."

WELCOME, Baby Margaret,
    From the golden shores of God—
Little pearl of comfort set
    In bereavèd Motherhood.

7

WITH TERPSICHORE.

THE NATIONAL DANCES—WALTZ.

[German movement, with Florentine Chanson—Anacreontic.]

ONE-*two-three, one-two-three*,
    Drain the grace-cup with me— -
Waltzing, sweet waltzing is love's oratory—so
    One-two-three, one-two-three,
    Drain the grace-cup with me—
Let old Fame, let old Fame have all her glory—O!
    One-two-three, one-two-three,
    Drain the grace-cup with me,
Let old War, let old War, have all his victory.
    One-two-three, one-two-three,
    Drain the grace-cup with me—
Give us sweet Bacchus and tripping Terpsichore!

VESUVIENNE.

(FRENCH MOVEMENT.)

WHAT is love but a dream?
    What is fame but a chance?
What is toil but a scheme?
What is life but a dance?—
    To the right now, to the left now,
    To the right now again.
Then trip with me, skip with me
    Over the green!

What is sighing but sin?
What is grieving but wrong?
The heart that would win
Must carry a song—
   To the right now, to the left now,
      To the right now again.
Then sigh no more, cry no more,
   On my heart lean,
And trip with me, skip with me
   Over life's green.

POLKA.*

(BOHEMIAN MOVEMENT.)

One-and two-and-three-and-four-and
One, two, three, four,

DANC'D a wicked peasant girl
   All on a Sunday's eve.
The schoolmaster so charmèd was,
He set the dance to bars, alas—
   Now would you it believe,
      And would you it believe!—
He slipt it off to Paristown,
Where Prague, that master of renown,
   Danced it before the wicked world
      All on a Sunday's eve.

It soon became a great *encore*,
This *one-and-two-and-three-and-four*,
   One, two, three, four,
And would you it believe,

* According to Czosnowski.

Now would you it believe?
It swept the town in seven days
And soon became the nation's craze,
    And even skipt the Atlantic wave
    And—*would you it believe?*—
Old Ocean did to listen stop,
    While hemispheres lockt arms to rock
This *one-and-two-and-three-and-four-and*
    One, two, three, four,
This dance the wicked peasant girl
Made on a Sunday's eve.

MAZOURKA.

(POLISH MOVEMENT.)

Tune, "*Black Key Mazourka.*"

Bi–e–lá–ski, Sar–bi–ews'–ki, Mà–sal–ski, and
                            Se–mi–ens'–ki.

THOSE renownèd Polish poets whom
            we all adore,
Decided they would fashion,
                fashion,
In honor of the nation,
                nation,
A dance of such gyration—
                —ration
    As never was danced before.

One-and-two-and-three-and-four-and,
One-and-two· and-three-and-four-and,
One-and-two-and-three-and-four-and,
    One, two, three, four.

When with a dedication,
                    —cation,
They gave it to the nation,
                    nation,
With Pole-to-Pole gyration,
                    —ration,
    It made a great *furor*.

It soon became the fashion,
                    fashion,
And all the wide creation,
                    —ation,
With mighty acclamation,
                    —mation
        Gave to it the floor,—
This *one-and-two-and-three-and-four-and, etc.*

FISHER'S HORNPIPE.

(SCOTTISH MOVEMENT.)

COME all ye sighing lasses, while old Time
        So slily passes—
He is filching all your roses while you
        Sigh your hearts away,—
Come let your wee feet twinkle to
        My hurdy-gurdy's tinkle,
Or with crow's feet he will wrinkle you
        And sprinkle you with gray.

Unbind your bonnie tresses to the
                Laddies' soft caresses—
They have sigh'd for you and cried
        For you and all but died away,—

Let your double feet now twinkle
     To my hurdy-gurdy's tinkle,
Or with crow's feet Time will wrinkle
     You and sprinkle you with gray.

RAQUET.

(AMERICAN MOVEMENT.)

COME, love, and glide with me—
     Over the bowling green,
One-two and one-two-three—
     Hearts and hands are clean.

Sweet blows the myrtle tree,
     Stars shine down serene—
One-two and one-two-three—
     Over the bowling green.

Bright seems the world to me
     When on my heart you lean—
One-two and one-two three—
     Hearts and hands are clean.

Then come, love, and dwell with me—
     Be my spirit's queen—
Come glide thro' life with me
     Over the bowling green—
One-two and one-two-three,
     Over the bowling green.

WITH THALIA.

A WORD FOR SAPPHO.

A WORD for Sappho.   Not to pæan
  Her suicide for love of Phaon—
A slanderous myth ! research will prove—
Not but sweet Sappho died of love,
But died as Hugo says to do it :
" *To die of love is to live thro' it.*"

  Thus Sappho died of love for Phaon ;
  Wherefore I lift mine humble pæan
  To prove the Sapphic head was level,
  Tho' Sapphic feet in strophe revel.

True, into exile was she sent,
But there are poets most content—
I doubt me not sweet Sappho *went.*

  Exiled from what ? "The vulgar herd."
  At home with the Sicilian bird,
  She stroll'd the sylvan solitude,
  And nurs'd her soft erotic mood,
  And harp'd an Aphroditean ode
To thrill the coming centuries' blood,
And drew from heaven such pure satire
As set the classic globe on fire,
And right and left such strophes hurl'd
As set a measure for the world !

Whilst Phaon, I dare say, crept apart
And died, man-like, of a broken heart!
Or haply 'twas his neck he broke
Leaping from that " Leucadian rock "—
On fame his solitary claim
That once sweet Sappho smiled on him—
That peerless gem of Mytillene
Who smiles thro' century-mists serene.

To-day all poets to Sappho fly
Who would artistically sigh,
All lovers true to Sappho hie
When they would classically "die."
For, know, as doth a poet behoove,
The peerless Sappho died of love—
But died as Hugo says to do it :
" *To die of love is to live thro' it.*"

JAMESTOWN WEED'S REVENGE.
A COMEDY OF TWO CONTINENTS.
IN FIVE ACTS.
ACT I.

JAMESTOWN weed sprung up in the corn
   Down at the edge of a Georgia cornfield ;
She wrapp'd her 'round with a prickly shield—
Said she, " I am proud, tho' I be low-born.
   Let the rabble corn stretch forth, if it will,
   Its tassel'd head and its welcoming arms ;
   I will hide from the vulgar world my charms,
   And never my heart shall they grind in the
      mill "—
                        Said Jamestown Weed.

Now a great dame, come from a foreign land,
Pass'd one day thro' the Georgia cornfield ;
And Jamestown Weed threw up her shield
And lifted her lily cup in her hand.
    The great dame paused, 'twixt a smile and a
      frown,
    Half in scorn, half ecstasy—
    " I will carry you home to Londontown
    And enter you into Society,"
                The great dame said.

Act II.

Now in Londontown they do wonderful things.
I am told that, without impropriety,
In their great Hothouse of Society,
They cultivate angels—just minus the wings.

There they rob Autumn's bosom of flowers for
    Spring's,
In October's hair they stick daffodowndillies,
Old Winter they deck out in roses and lilies—
O, in Londontown they do wonderful things !

Man has taken the weather out of God's hands,
And storm and tide pass under his rod
As they used to yield to the beckon of God—
They have only to loosen Orion's bands
            In Londontown.

Oh ! you never had known poor Jamestown Weed,
Had you seen her there with her proud arch'd neck
And her lovely complexion with never a speck
Nor a freckle to mar,—and her well-pois'd head.

And her Queen Anne collar of velvety green,
And her mantle she stood so statelily in,
Fastened about her with never a pin!—
Ah! but she looked like a very born queen.

Poor Jamestown Weed! had you only but held
Your breath when the great dame ventured the touch
Of her blueblooded nose—you might now have swelled
On that great dame's breast 'neath a diamond brooch.

But barely her highness had lifted you up
Than over her senses the memory came
Of a prickly weed and a vulgar name
And a noxious draught from a cornfield cup.

And so to the pavement she fillipt you down,
With an air of contempt, " O blood will tell!
That vulgar, that vile *continental smell !*
'Twas folly to bring you to Londontown ! "
                              The great dame said.

Better to be in the cornfield still,
Poor Jamestown Weed! hiding under the corn—
Better by far to have never been born—
Or to have your heart ground up in the mill,
                              Poor Jamestown Weed.

Act III.

Now the great dame's Doctor, chancing that way,
Slipt his heel upon Jamestown Weed,
So as to make her poor heart bleed,
Red blood mixed with an English gray.

First some very undoctorly words he said,
Then his pellet eyes rolled in visions of glory,
"I will carry you home to my laboratory,
And make you in pellets to raise the dead"—
That Doctor said.

Act IV.

Now that very same day, so the townspeople tell it,
The great dame, seized with a violent rack
All down her chest and her neck and her back,
Sends for her Doctor to fly with a pellet.

And the Doctor is there in a cat's eye-winking
(For when great dames call good doctors come
      quick),
And he finds the great dame sick, very sick—
Indeed the great dame is rapidly sinking.

" Quick, Doctor! good Doctor! I'm dying fast!"
So Jamestown Weed in her little coat
Of sugar slips down that great dame's throat,
Saying, " Oho! my time has come at last!"

The great dame's Doctor is holding his breath,
And the great dame is clutching the good Doctor
      tight.
Says Jamestown Weed, "Shall I kill her outright,
Or shall I make it a lingering death?"

Now she doubled her up—now she soothed her a spell,
But the very next moment, so I have been told
(For weeds sometimes have hearts of gold),
The great dame sprang to her feet sound-well!

"O Doctor! what wonderful pill have we here!"
" *Stramonium*, madam—the more vulgar name
Is ' *Jimson*,' a field-weed "—But here the great dame
Sends a shriek thro' the rafters, " O dear! and O
  Dear!!—

" That weed with the vile *continental smell!*
I picked up and foolishly thought to refine—
Do you mean, sir, to say *I have taken her in ?* "
And back in the bed in a spasm she fell.

"Not so fast!" said the Doctor, well-arm'd in a
  minute—
" It is not so bad as it seems to be—
You have swallow'd one of the F. F. V.,
With a strain of the real Pocahontas blood in it!"

ACT V.

Passers by now observe in the great dame's boudoir
A pale stately bloom, which she calls *Queen de Lis*,
And kisses in passing, and makes *pot-pourri*
Of its leaves, as they fall, for her jewel'd rose-jar.

Her good doctor now she needs never to call,
And she cares less and less for Society,
As she gives all her heart to her sweet protégé—
Whose breeding dates back as far as St. Paul.

PRETTY CAPRICE.

(Capra: A Goat)

PRETTY Caprice rusht down to the lake
  To drown herself for love's own sake;
  For her lover was false, they said,
  And why not, then, be dead ?

Pretty Caprice had not rusht far
  When she stumpt her toe on a broken jar,
    And hoppt back to the house to have
    It doctor'd with Grandpa's salve.

Pretty Caprice got just to the door
  When she thought of her visit to the poor
    That she had not made that week—
    So she hasten'd her basket to seek.

Pretty Caprice on her way to the cupboard,
  Espying her cheese-cloth Mother Hubbard,
    Straightway began to gape,
    And crawled to her room for a nap.

Now pretty Caprice had done all this
  And twenty things else, the notional miss,
    When unto her mind it occurr'd
    That maybe her neighbor had err'd—

Yes! the envious thing! she had slander'd her lover!
  So she snatcht up her hat and the street hurried over,
    To challenge Miss Emma Lou Gray—
    To a two-handed game of croquet.

BALLADE OF THE LITTLE CORNER.
(Dedicated to My Mother.)

SHE is just a little corner
  Of red Atlanta clay;
Too long to fit a sonnet
And too homely for a lay,
But I love her; yes, I love her,
And I'll put her in my tome,
Because this little corner
Is the key to mother's home.

Some call her "little shoestring,"
Some call her "little snag,"
Some call her "little matchbox,"
Some call her "little thorn ;"
She's a modest little corner,
And she knows not how to brag.
And she has too little brea'th, alas!
To blow her own horn:
So she just accepts these titles,
And holds on to her own,
And some day, *a la* Paul, she may
Become the chiefest stone.

She's a quiet little corner,
But when she needs to speak
She can use the German language,
Or the Latin, or the Greek ;
But generally lets others talk
And hides her blushing cheek,
And goes on with her business
In a manner mild and meek.

She's a fruitful little corner,
And annually bears
Ten carloads of bananas
And five thousand crates of pears ;
Not to mention little lunches
Of bread and salad made,
And such harmless little punches
As sweet milk and lemonade.

She's a pious little corner
And careth not for pelf,
And loves her gentle neighbors
Even as she loves herself ;

And she would not, could she help it,
Stand in anybody's light,
Nor be a pebble of offence,
  For that's
        Not
            Right.

Some day she may sink out of sight
(An earthquake happening by),
And then again she may shoot up
And all but kiss the sky;
There is no telling now, you know,
About these little corners—
Some day she may pull up a plum
As big as Jacky Horner's.

Meanwhile I'll go on weaving
Little lyrics to adorn her;
For some day Pussy's sure to come,
And "Pussy wants a corner."
But if she wants it badly
She will have to wait and labor,
And sing that psalm of life that sprung
From dear Longfellow's Faber—
For this timid little corner
Might say,
      "Next
         Door
            Neighbor."

She's a happy little corner.
Once she stood all alone,
With no strong arm to support her,
And she made a hollow moan,

Until an admiring neighbor
Saw her unprotected side
And offered her his hand and purse—
"Pray, would she be his bride?"
She responded, blushing coyly,
"There's such difference in our heights—
But I'll let you stand beside me—
For I'm not a 'woman's rights'—
I'll be a sister to you,
And you can be my brother—
I can't promise to obey you,
For—I'm promised to another."
So once again she's swimming
On fortune's tidal wave,
And her grateful heart is brimming
For this kind support he gave.

Yes, she's just a little corner
Of red Atlanta clay,
Too long to fit a sonnet,
And too homely for a lay;
But I love her; yes, I love her,
And I'll put her in my tome,
For this precious little corner
Is the key to mother's home.

ALBOIN AND ROSAMOND.

HIGH run the revel. 'Round the spacious board
Capacious bowls of Bacchus sparkling pour'd.
"The skull of Cunnimund!" Alboin cried.
A courtier instant placed it at his side.
A ghastly sight! yet splendid—where once beam'd
The warrior's eyes, two blood-red rubies gleam'd.

All rimm'd around it was with Ophir's gold,
The royal coat-of-arms thereon inscroll'd.
(Alboin's hand it was had laid him low,
In jealousy of Rosamond's devotion.)   *"Now
Bid my fair spouse,"* he cried, *" the feast to join,
From her mourn'd sire's skull to sip sweet wine."*
With agonizing rage cag'd in her breast,
Fair Rosamond obeisance thus exprest :
" Thy will, my liege, my privilege 'tis to obey ;"
But e'er her lips, all quivering, touch'd the clay,
A silent vow they made, the insult should
That day be wiped out with Alboin's blood.

The banquet o'er, the Emperor, drows'd with drink,
Betakes him to his couch, in rest to sink.
His anxious spouse, to insure her lord's repose,
Charges the palace guard the gates to close ;
Now sinks beside his couch and smoothes his tresses,
Till slumber falls, allur'd by soft caresses.
But barely into Lethe hath he glided
When, lo ! the silken arras are divided—
Out slip the affrighted colleagues, all in mask,
Urg'd straight to execute their heinous task.
Now, at her signal, at his side they crouch.   [couch,
The Emperor, warn'd in dreams, springs from his
His hand upon his trusty broadsword laid—
But, lo ! the scabbard fails to yield the blade.
The hand of Rosamond hath made it fast—
And smiling now she sees him breathe his last.
And to this day the world hath to decide,
Which is in infamy the deeper dyed—
The Emperor, Alboin, or his bride.

8

IN ZION.

"IN THE DAYS OF MY YOUTH."

An Invocation.

PREPARE me, O God, for the day Thou hast
　　spoken,
When the daughters of music shall be brought low,
When the voice of a bird shall rise up as a token
And the sound of the grinding be distant and low,
The silver cord loos'd, and the golden bowl broken,
And earth's pleasant fountains with bitterness flow.

In the days of my youth let me heed life's conclu-
　　sion,
Ere dust unto dust I return to the sod;
My will against thine were presumptuous obtrusion,
Soon to my long home passing under thy rod—
'Tis the whole of man's duty—all else is confusion—
To love Thee and keep Thy commandments, O God.

Not the making of books be my task without end-
　　ing—
There is but one book, e'en the Book of Thy Word—
But a song from a heart to be ever upsending
With praises toward heaven, like the song of a bird,
That haply some wand'rer may cease his offending,
To list to my lay. and so turn to his Lord.

WHEN FIRST I ESSAY'D ON MY UNTUTOR'D LYRE.

WHEN first I essay'd on my untutor'd lyre
 To lift to Thee, O Pure and Undefiled,
A psalm, I falter'd out, like Jeremiah,
 "Lord God, I cannot speak—I am a child."

Then came a gentle voice, "Be not afraid—
 My influence shall hover o'er thy hand."
Before my angel I bow'd low my head,
 And sang as inspiration gave command.

Unto my psalm I said, "O let thy feet
 Be swift and beautiful upon the mount,
As one who brings suspense glad tidings sweet,
 Or stricken thirst cool pitchers from a fount.

Ah! might'st thou woo one troubled soul to lean
 More surely on His grace, my task were done."
"Nay!" interpos'd my angel, with serene
 Assurance, "it were only just begun."

CHRIST THE LIVING WATER.

ANTHEM.

HO! every one that thirsteth, come ye to the foun-
 tain
 And drink the living water freely given;
  Come ye that have no money
  And get you wine and honey,
And eat the bread of life that cometh only down
 from heaven.

O whyfore spend ye money for that which is not
　　substance ?
　　Why labor ye for that which cannot fill,
　　　　While wine of inspiration
　　　　For every pure ambition
Outgusheth here in plenteous founts from Zion's holy
　　hill ?

Ye who have some secret sorrow that recoileth from
　　the daylight—
　　Perchance some fleshly idol turn'd to stone—
　　　　Here give your cross expression,
　　　　Here unbosom your confession
And hide your sorrow's ashes in the rock whence ye
　　were hewn.

Come all ye toiling multitudes, ye weeders of the
　　vineyard,
　　Who sweat while idle worldings sleep or parley,
　　　　Come to this fount of blessing,
　　　　Of mercy never ceasing,
And get wheat instead of thistles, and instead of
　　cockle, barley.

Come all ye that mourn in Zion, here is beauty for
　　your ashes,
　　Here is liberty for captives of the sword—
　　　　With the oil of joy anoint you,
　　　　And, as Heaven did appoint you,
Be ye as trees of righteousness, the planting of the
　　Lord.

Have ye battled with the footmen ? have ye wrestled
　　with the horsemen ?

Have ye put your trust in chariots and been
    thrown ?
       Here the helmet of salvation
       Will protect you from the passion
Of the swelling of the Jordan when " the wakeful
    trump " is blown.

Come all ye weary-laden, drink the living water freely ;
    The Spirit and the Bride say, Come.
       Come every one that heareth
       And (the Spirit witness beareth)
Be ye beautified and " clothed upon " with your
    celestial home.

And the prickly thorn will vanish for the fir-tree's
    glad upspringing,
And where crept the brier will spread the myrtle-tree,
       And while pæans to Heav'n are winging,
       And while Heaven-harps are ringing,
       And while chapel-bells are swinging,
       Mount Zion will burst forth singing,
And the echoing little hills will skip and clap their
    hands for glee.

TO-DAY'S GETHSEMANE.

ALONE on heaven-heights His Spirit dwelt,
    What time on earth He laid His healing touch,
And O, I think His loneliness was such
As human isolation never felt.

But came an hour when, tempted and earth-weary,
He stole apart unto Gethsemane,
With Peter and the sons of Zebedee,
There to uplift his night-long *miserere*.

But while He prayed, they off to slumber crept,
"The faithful three"—aye, while He lifted up
His eyes to God's White Throne and drained His
      cup
Of passion, they—even they, His disciples—slept.

Even so I think that He to-day may weep
In memory of earth's Gethsemane,
To see his churches, like "The faithful three,"
When most He needs them, creeping off to sleep.

EASTER ANTHEM.

O LOOK ye! the floral apostles are spreading
    A scroll of glad tidings o'er earth's desert
      places—
A psalm beatific, in signs hieroglyphic,
All writ by the roses and lilies and daisies.
      Listen! listen! Christ is risen!
Sing the new heavens and the new earth.
    Old things to-day are vanish'd away—
      The risen Christ hath birth.

The little lambs heed it and o'er the hills speed it,
The happy hills pass it apace to the trees,
The trees clap it forward to birds soaring starward,
And the heavens rediamond it over the seas.
      Listen! listen! Christ is risen!
Sing the new heavens and the new earth.
    Old things to-day are vanish'd away,
      The risen Christ hath birth.

THE TREE I LOVE.

[Set to Music by H. B. Augustine, of Elgin, Ill.]

Ps. lii. 8.

IN the house of my God many trees there are,
　On the banks of the Beautiful River,—
Cedars of Lebanon, rich and rare;
The Tree of Life, whose broad leaves are
For the healing of nations; the fig tree, too,
Once wither'd by Truth, now by Truth made new.
But the tree I love in the sacred sod
On the banks of the Beautiful River
Is the tree where the sweet tired Psalmist stood
In his harp's *selah*, with soul a-quiver,
Is the green olive tree in the house of my God.
And I trust in His mercy forever and ever.

KING DAVID DANCED.

FROM Obed-Edom brought they out
　The ark of God with joyful shout.
　In sooth it was a goodly sight!
　" Before the Lord," with all his might,
King David danced, King David danced.

Six goodly oxen did they kill—
　　King David danced,
And blood of fatlings freely spill—
　　King David danced.
With linen ephod girt about,
With trumpet sound and joyful shout,
What time from Obed-Edom out
They brought the ark, King David danced.

With sackbut, psaltery and cymbal,
With tabret, pan-pipes, horn and timbrel,
They play'd a merry roundabout,
And rais'd on high a joyful shout—
        King David danced.

Michal, Saul's daughter, heard the shout,
And from her window glancëd out—
        King David danced !
    She righteously did criticise him,
    " And in her heart she did despise him "—
        King David danced.
As Noah danc'd before his ark,
As Bacchus in the ages dark,
    He leap'd in wildest revelry—
    He skipt, he leapt, he reel'd, he pranc'd,
    Alas for human frailty !
        King David danced.
But when in after years we see
Him bow'd down in his agony,
And making deep and ceaseless moan,
" O Absalom, my son, my son !
Would God that I had died for thee ! "
Or wrestling with his enemies,
Who compass him about with lies,
Whose tongues were butter, and whose words,
Softer than oil, were yet drawn swords ;
Or, later, 'neath the olive tree
Confessing his humility,
" Even as a weanëd child I be,"
And trusting God, with lips that quiver,
" Henceforth forever and forever."
Still later 'neath the Almighty shade
Abiding, calm, and unafraid

Of fowler's snare or arrow's flight
Or terrors that invade the night,
Trampling the dragon 'neath his feet,
Praising God's loving-kindness great,
Lifting on high his confidence,
Unterrorized by the advance
Of the night-creeping pestilence,
While at his right hand thousands fall,
And at his left ten thousand—all
Our indignation melts away
Like mist before the rising day;
We honor him and love him so,
That we forgive his phrenzied shout
What time from Obed-Edom out
They brought the ark of God—we lean
On his strong harp and say, What tho',
When on his knees he should have been,
      King David danced !

GOD MAKETH A WAY.

FOR him who is fain to see the light
    God maketh a way, God maketh a way.
Came Nicodemus in the night,
    Zealous Zaccheus climb'd the tree,
      Some are so reverential that
      They have only need to watch and wait.
For him who is fain to see the light,
For him who is fain to do the right,
    God maketh a way.

HYMN.

FATHER Omnipotent,
    All-good, all-glorious,
O'er mortal discord
Thy peace is victorious.

O Thou omniscient,
Holy and perfect One,
Teach us to image Thee
Thro' thy beloved Son.

Our earthly idols we
Too long have serv'd—unbound,
Now, like the Prodigal,
Husks lying all around,

Humbly to Thee we turn,
Thy mercy-seat to prove,—
Darkness and death below,
Light and thy grace above.

Take our unworthiness,
All that we have to give,
Be to us what we lack,
Lift us near Thee to live.

And when earth's veil is rent
And at Thy throne we kneel,
Set on our ransom'd brows
Thine apostolic seal.

Father Omnipotent,
All-good, all-glorious,
O'er mortal discord
Thy peace is victorious.

O Thou omniscient,
Holy and perfect One,
Teach us to image Thee
Thro' thy beloved Son.

JORDAN.

DEEP-SWELLING, muddy, turbulent—
   A noise between two silences—
'Twixt Alpha and Omega bent,
A channel for inharmonies.

Upon thy desolate banks to-day
No lofty citadels arise,
No forests spread their majesty
To mark thine ancient victories.

What mad ambition could have bent
Thy curious path, like Satan coiled ?—
For doth not Jeremiah lament,
" How is the pride of Jordan spoil'd ! "

Here Joshua cleav'd thee with his host—
Surely some giant palm must fling
Its shade here—nay ! a nitrous crust,
Thro' which no grassblade dare upspring.

Once o'er the desert came a Voice,
" Make straight the pathway of the Lord ! "
But thou pursued'st thy sinuous choice,
Unmindful of the sacred Word.

Lo, here the dear baptismal spot,
The " Bathing Place " of pilgrim fame—
Ah, Bethabara, one had not
Known thee but for thy treasur'd name.

'Twas here the Pure and Undefiled,
By way of apostolic grace,
Humbling him as a little child,
Suffer'd thy wave to sweep His face.

Certes here blows some asphodel,
Some lily-bloom, to mark the place
Where the baptismal water fell
In sacred drops from His pure face.

Nay! slime pits, thermal springs, and thistle,
A few weird stalks of hollyhock,
While overhead the bitterns whistle,
Or nest in crags of basalt rock.

O basest of ingratitude,
Not to outblossom here thy thanks!
But to blaspheme thy bitterest mood
Against thy cold, unconscious banks.

And must we cross thee in the end,
Dark Jordan—brave thy mysteries,
Or ere our ransom'd souls ascend
The sacred Beulah-heights of bliss?

If in the land of peace wherein
We trusted, we have weariedly
Let fall the oars on waves serene,
How shall we ford thee in that day?—

Deep-swelling, muddy, in eclipse,
A noise between two silences—
'Twixt Genesis and Apocalypse,
A channel for inharmonies.

IN THE MOUNTAINS OF NORTH GEORGIA.

MIDNIGHT ON THE BALD.

'TIS midnight on "the Bald"—
   And O! for Poe and power—
In a fine rage on Fancy's page
   To flash this matchless hour.

Lo, where the raven Night
   Doth flap her ebon wing,
And o'er the edge of the hoar Blue Ridge
   Cimmerian shadows fling—

Now from 'neath beetling brows
   A lancèd summons thrust,
Rallying the winds from the earth's four ends
   To meet in tournament-joust.

Hist, where they come in a trice!—
   Boreas, Cyclops-wheel'd,
The foaming East, and the panting West,
   With the eye of Jove in his shield!—

And—bravest afield, I trow—
   With shy Eolian sallies,
The low-voic'd South, with her roseate mouth,
   Trippeth it over the valleys.

Georgia and Tennessee,
   The Carolina twins,
And old Alabama, gaze on the drama
   From the surrounding plains.

It all began in sport,
   As many a joust of yore,
In round-table days, but it endeth in craze
   And fuel and duel and gore!

"Blood Mountain" gappeth afresh,
   There on her scar-seam'd side;
And "Double Knobs," with throes and sobs,
   Opeth his hell-gates wide.

Thrice do I see a head
   Of Cerberus protrude,
Thrice hear a bark, thro' the lurid dark,
   Of hell-hounds thirsting blood.

With a voiceless prayer I turn
   And lean up thro' the skies
To the seventh Heaven; and my soul is shriven
   Straightway of its agonies.

Joy! and the world is God's—
   The sweet South is prevailing!—
And calm on the breast of the rainbow'd West,
   Queen Cynthia is sailing.

CYNTHIA.

CYNTHIA! next woman best-lov'd of my muse,
   Whose smile, discovering hers, is all I ask
To prove that heaven sometimes deigns to earth—
Celestial Arbitress! who in the same
Undeviate path mine infant vision traced,
Pursuest even now thy smiling course
How dost thou teach a lesson to my soul
Of perseverance and of constancy!

Who callest thee inconstant doth but view
Thee superficially—a narrow thought !—
Let him but turn back contemplation's eye
Upon thine ancient record, and he stands
Abash'd at his misjudgment.
                        Fail'st thou yet
Ever to bring the seasons in due course
Of sequence, throughout all the centuried years
That thou hast calendar'd in the tome of time ?
Ever to welcome in the marching months,
Each at his several mile-post, in their rounds
Zodiacal ? To pour thy pitying urn
Of balm on January's winding-sheets ?
To wave o'er February's *miserere*
Thy crystal wand of promise ? with calm gaze
To charm the savage breast of lion March
To lamblikeness ? to float thy crescent arc
O'er April's flood-tide of despondency ?
In sweet May's hyacynthine locks to set
A silver comb ? to shed thine influence
In gracious streams on June, thy chosen one ?
To throw an odorous spray of pearly dews
On July's feverish pillow? or to press
To August's parchèd lips an ample urn
Of golden nectar ? 'Round September's shrine
To softly swing an incense lamp of prayer ?
To spread a benediction-halo round
October's brow, as o'er the harvest fields
Rejoicingly she came forth, bringing sheaves ?
To badge November's melancholy breast
With opaline insignia of hope ?
To pin with topaz brooch December's cloak
About his shivering limbs as he went down
The tottering steep to fill his vault of ice ?

Or fail'st thou ever yet to bring the tide
At the appointed hour back to the shore
Expectant?   Nay; not even when thou dost hide
The favor of thy countenance from this spot
Infinitesimal of God's universe,
That holds our horoscope, even while thy smile
Charmeth our sister hemisphere, thy thought
Is for our vantage and protection.

Inconstant!   Thou art constancy's own mould.
What tho' thou proteanly adjust thy mood
To suit thy journeying's convenience?
Thy very phases are reliable
And spring not unawares, but rather greet
The anticipatory eye, outwearied with
The unvarying roundness of the heavenly host.
What time thou'rt "new," thy crescent symboleth
    hope;
What time thou'rt "waxing," thou'rt developing,
As interesting things must needs be doing;
We admire thy "half" for that we miss thy whole;
Thy glorious " full " doth challenge optic skill
By any common measurement to gauge
Its puzzling amplitude, as it doth mount
The horizontal distance, backgrounding
Acres of forests, or outlining clear
Against its blaze some dim cathedral tower;
Thy "wane "—ah! thou art loveliest on the wane,
As all earth's blessings are.   How oft we cheat
The midnight couch of sleep to watch thee waste
Thy lovely self away in heaven's wilds,
As thou wert grown aweary of the world
In all its curtain'd sinfulness, and would'st
Withdraw into thy grave-clothes, lest thou shame,

By lingering here, Diana's memory.
Thy day-ghost fascinates me most of all—
The very height of its audacity !
To face day's very monarch on his throne
And smiling say, I borrowed beams of thee
All thro' the night, and now I lend thee back
These borrow'd rays to help thee light the day !

Sweet Cynthia, empress of my dreams ! what tho'
Thou'rt but a satellite ? since thou dost tend
Thy part of th' empyrean vineyard well :
Remove his satellite, our sun is shorn
Of half his glory—'twere to clip
His locks ambrosial on his midnight couch.
What tho' 'neath scientific scrutiny
Thy heart be hollow and thy face be scarred
With ancient warfare ?   What tho' on thy brow
Old Superstition hath instamp'd a man
Forever burning brush ? The poet's eye
Seeth thee only as the Lady Moon,
Fickle, but ever thro' thy fickleness
Unchanging, constant thro' inconstancy,
Consistent e'en in inconsistency,
A charming paradoxical mystery.
I know a lady so—I love her well—
Rely upon her utterly, and wait
With tender interest her to-and-fro
Excursions o'er my being's horoscope.
Like Bailey's " Festus " and like thee, fair Queen !
She is inconsistent—"so was meant to be"—
Hath flung away that overrated jewel,
Consistency (if e'er she wore it) for
That pearl of greater price, humility.

9   .

Aye, me! sweet Cynthia—dost leave me so,
In very height of rapport with thy charms?
'Tis like thee!   Dost thou with nereidian grace
Mount yonder sea-horse cloud and bound away
O'er billowy waves of foam just touched with rose
By Aurora's finger-tips—dost bound and sink
Down, down into the liquid depths of space,
Leaving behind a silver trail of peace?
Ah! well—'tis well! Thou hast left me thus before.
Nay! there she floateth—see her silver crest
Just rising o'er the foam! she turneth half
Her face to me in lingering farewell—
Her lady face! for modern fancy hath
Rebell'd 'gainst ancient superstition,
Outpluck'd the man and cameo'd there instead
A lady's classic profile—so I toss
Thee *au revoir*, sweet Cynthia, on this kiss.

OLD FATHER CORN.

FOURSCORE, and feeble of limb,
    He sits in his vine-wreath'd door,
And smiles and croons his melodious hymn,
    Blest like the hermits of yore.

Over a life well spent,
    He broods with pious pride,
His residue of days content
    To rest in the mountain side.

Within a radius 'round
    Of thirty miles his legions
Of Baptist tracts have strewn the ground
    Of these benighted regions.

Aye, every desert place,
  And bottom-ground plantation,
Can boast its sinner brought to grace
  Under his exhortation.

And every mountain-crag
  Hath echoed back his thunder,
And every creek at least may brag
  One sinner dipp'd down under

By good old Father Corn.
  Long may this gray-hair'd voyager
Live to illumine and adorn
  The mountains of North Georgia.

SONG OF A MOUNTAIN MAIDEN.

SAPPHO'S hair was black as night,
  When the night is gloomiest;
Helen's like a tuft of bright
  Golden-rod when plumiest:
But nor Sappho in Mytilene,
  Nor Helen yet at Troy,
Had hair so full of joy, I ween,
  So full of Keats's joy—
So beautiful forevermore,
  So tender, so myrrh-laden,
As Ida's gloaming hair—my rare,
  My matchless mountain maiden!

Juno's eyes were sapphire-blue,
  Dante's Beatrice's
Chrysolite, and aquamarine
  Algernon's Felice's;

But, nor the orbs of Jove's delight,
   Of Dante's inspiration,
Nor Swinburne's guiding stars serene,
   Could glint a scintillation
(More magical than ever flasht
   From lantern of Aladdin),
Like Ida's diamond eyes—my rare,
   My matchless mountain maiden!

Laura's lips were nectar-red,
   Meet for Petrarch's kisses;
Sweet to Swift were Stella's, sweet
   To Waller Sacharisse's;
But nor the lips that Petrarch bless'd,
   Nor those that made the Dean glad,
Nor those that warbling Waller press'd,
   Such fountain's nectarine had,
A poet's spirit to refresh,
   A poet's heart to gladden,
As Ida's Eden lips—my rare,
   My matchless mountain maiden!

EYES.

(TO MUSIC.)

EYES that dartle, eyes that dare—
   O the glory of them!
Eyes that startle when I draw near,
   Seeing how I love them—
Startle and droop and tremble,
   And all but shut out my bliss—
Then—eyes that cannot dissemble—

Draw me in with a kiss,
    Sweet eyes !
Draw me in with a kiss.

Eyes that weave for me mystic spells,
    Eyes that are deep and fearful,
Eyes that could drown me in their wells,
    If they were not too careful—
That carry me down, down, down,
    In love's divine baptism,
Only to lift me and crown
    Me at last with love's bright prism,
        Pure eyes !
At last with love's bright prism.

Eyes that soften and glint and glow,
    Like sun-shot dewdrops golden ;
Eyes that could pierce me thro' and thro'
    Were they not love-beholden—
Pierce me and turn me and chill me,
    And send me adrift—alone—
Eyes that could leave me—and kill me,
    If they were not mine own
        True eyes !
If they were not mine own.

MELODIES IN MINOR KEY.

ROSEMARY AND RUE.

"Rosemary, that's for remembrance."—Shakespeare.
"Rue, herb of grace."—Jeremy Taylor.

I HAVE a friend.   But one behoves.
　　I hold it true, on this sad earth,
　　One friend a sea of friends is worth.
Friends change.   A friend at all times loves.

To thee—my Friend—at all times true—
　　Whose wound is faithful as thy kiss,
　　I offer, in deep tenderness,
This ring of rosemary and rue,

From memory-meadows cull'd, on calm
　　And solitary starlight eves,
　　And press'd away 'twixt sacred leaves,
Their bitter-sweet to waxen balm.

"That's for remembrance "—" Rose of Mary,"
　　Meet emblem of fidelity ;
　　And rue, sad flower, worn anciently
At penitential *miserere*.

A crown of bay-leaves might I send,
　　Of honor redolent and success—
　　But nay ! I ween ' twere valued less
Than this pale wreath.   Take it, my Friend,—

Not on thy silver locks to set,—
　　Thy threescore years of gentle deeds
　　A softer halo 'round thee sheds
Than ever stream'd from coronet :

Not as my gratitude's return
　　For grace beyond all guerdoning ;
　　But as a simple memory-ring
To hang on Friendship's golden urn.

PERSIAN SERENADE.

[Set to music by Edward Von Adelung, of Oakland, Cal.]

IN no sadder strain than these
　　Lugubrious minor keys
The bulbul wooes the climbing rose, O Sweet !
Yet still to my soft pleading
Thou turn'st an ear unheeding,
And wonderest why pride lets me linger at thy feet.
　　　　Sweetheart !　Sweetheart !
　　　　Why avert those perfect eyes ?
　　　　Sweetheart !　Sweetheart !
　　　　Take me into Paradise.

Ah ! would for one fleet hour
I were the climbing flower,
And thou the Persian bulbul perch'd upon my stem ;
In order thou might'st see
How sweeter 'tis to be
Prone at Love's feet than crown'd with Pride's pale
　　diadem.
　　　　Sweetheart !　Sweetheart !
　　　　Why avert those perfect eyes ?
　　　　Sweetheart !　Sweetheart !
　　　　Take me—take me into Paradise.

RAIN IN MIDSUMMER.

THE lowering skies were leaden-gray—
   My heart was leaden too.
"O love," I said, "when hope is dead,
   Which way to look?"—"Look up," he said.
But toward the earth I bent my head
(As you would do if hope were dead);
      And, unresisting,
      Kept on twisting
        Wreaths of rue.

The leaden skies were muttering now—
   My heart was muttering too.
"O love," I said, "when love is fled,
   Which way to look?"—"Look up," he said.
But lower still I bent my head
(As you had done with cheeks as red),
      And, still persisting,
      Kept on twisting
        Wreaths of rue.

The muttering skies were weeping now—
   My heart was weeping too.
"O love," I said, "if faith were dead,
   Which way to look?"—"Look up," he said.
And toward the skies I lift mine eyes
(As you had done had you been wise)—
      And lo! the riven
      Gates of heaven,
        Barr'd with blue.

THE SENSITIVE VISITOR.

THE night was bitter. Pride and I
　　Sat gazing at it thro' the pane.
Who can that bold intruder be
That at our casement draweth rein !

We turn our faces, Pride and I.
And yet—the pleading and the pain
Of that one look—Nay ! out of view
He's pass'd into the night and rain.

Who could that gallant horseman be ?
Alas ! to-day 'tis but too plain :
His name was *Opportunity*.
He never came to us again.

THE MEADOWLARK.

I LOVE our melancholy meadowlark ;
　　In dirge-like cadency it must excel
The transatlantic minion, Philomel.
It waiteth not the lonesome hour of dark
On its aerial voyage to embark,
And flood the world with a melodious knell
Of wailful minors, but its throat will swell
Even when the sun is at his dizziest mark
Of splendor, and the flowers with dew unwet,
And pour its mid-May woes into the heart
Of men and roses, lest they should forget
In even the sunniest life death plays a part.
O for a Keats ! in song to immortalize
This nightingale of our Columbian skies.

"THE PATH FROM ME TO THEE THAT LEADS."

THE path from me to thee that leads,
  With teary seed-pearls thick bestrewn,
Beneath some vernal silver moon
Will blossom out in fragrant deeds—

Not sorrow-thorns nor passion-tares,
For friendship soweth not such seeds,
But dreams come true and answer'd prayers—
The path from thee to me that leads.

UNDER THE LAUREL.

UNDER the laurel, last year's May,
  We sat and talked till the day went out,
And you bound my temples 'round about
With a wreath of roses twined with bay—
    Roses for love, and bay for fame—
    For the costliest treasure at life's command,
    A woman's heart, you had laid in my hand—
    And time would bring me a sounding name.
      Under the laurel, hush, ah hush !
      Memory lurks in the laurel bush.

Under the laurel breezes blow
Soft as they did in last year's spring,
But, oh ! what a different song they sing,
For, oh ! what a different tale they know.
    " Roses for love, and bay for fame."
    Under the laurel I sit alone
    And weave a wreath for a cold gravestone—
    And tiime has brought me the sounding name.
      Under the laurel, hush, ah hush !
      Memory lurks in the laurel bush.

BETWIXT THE MOUNTAIN AND THE MAIN.

BETWIXT the mountain and the main
   A cloud of mist is creeping—
And she is high, and he is low,
And both are softly sleeping.

She dreameth on love-restless couch
About her one true lover,
Who in his vessel silver-sail'd
The sea is speeding over.

He lieth 'neath the oozy wave,
But no deep bell is tolling.
Betwixt the mountain and the main
The cloud of mist is rolling.

The bursting sun, a signal glad,
Her couch is golding over;
She hasteth down the mountain slope
To meet her one true lover.

Betwixt the mountain and the main
The cloud of mist is parted—
And he is high, and she is low,
And which is happier-hearted?

FLORIDIAN NOCTURNE.

A MELLOWING moon—an immigrating wind,
   Laden with myrrh, that quickens in the pulse
A sense of Oriental tamarind,
Of golden cinnamon and purple dulse.

A fallow marshland—hints of wild florescence,
The cypress' green against the lemon's white;
While from palm-thicket comes melodious prescience
Of perfect days to be and full delight.

> O love, my love ! the days to be !—
> Faith's prescient eye hath seen—
> The days to be, for thee and me—
> What recks the might have been?

A shred of seaweed tangled in a pearl,
A sigh of seaweeds wafting a delight
To where the charitable clouds unfurl
And fold it evermore from human sight.

And is it well she lies so stilly calm,
With orange-buds twined in her hair's soft wave,
While earth fulfils the promise from the palm,
And stars and blossoms gleam above her grave?

> Aye, love, my love, the days to be !
> Faith's prescient eye hath seen—
> The days to be for thee and me
> Beyond the might have been.

LOVE'S WELCOMERS.

JOY and Sorrow (sisters they)
  Hand in hand, one close of day,
Walk'd the dappled meadows.
In Joy's footprints dewlights gleamed,
Sorrow's left behind, it seemed,
Only streams and shadows.

Much ado they had, I trow,
Keeping step—one quick, one slow,

One sad, one happy-hearted;
Yet they are so close of kin,
Being twin-born, 'twould seem a sin
If they should be parted.

" Welcome, Love!" they call together,
As the sweet boy bursts the ether
In the wake of Venus.
" Truth our sire sent us to meet you,
Truth our sire sent us to greet you,
And bring you home between us."

BALLAD OF THE BROKEN TROTH.

"AY me!" she shivering said,
    And gazed on the sunlit skies aboon,
Where, clasped in the scorching arms of noon,
There floated, cold and white,
The day-ghost of the waning moon,
    All in its hearse-shroud dight—
        All in its hearse-shroud dight.

"'Tis a passing thought," she said,
"Of last year's broken troth, I ween "
    (And I would ye had seen her white face then,
    Ye women who play with the hearts of men !),
"Which e'en as a mockery floats between
The rising and the setting
Of this year's love—what might have been,
        To keep me from forgetting—
            To keep me from forgetting."

" But I will forget," she said,
" Ere the rosebuds ope on another June."
And she warbled a snatch of lancers' tune,

Rounding it off with laughter.
But the pale cold day-ghost of the moon,
Wrapped in the scorching arms of noon,
Haunted her ever after—
Ever and ever after.

BETWEEN THE LINES.

"THE past cannot be changed."—No, dear,
But may be misinterpreted.
How many life-wrongs righted were
If this dim page aright we read!
If we could read between the lines
The acts of struggle, thoughts of grace
(Not limited by our confines
Of human judgment), how this space,
Illumined by a light above,
Would burst in beauties everywhere,
And we would blush at our self-love,
And marvel at our past despair—
Between the lines,
Between the lines,
To see the hidden graces there.

Then faithful to each fond ideal,
Let us, sweet friend, turn back in prayer
And there search out the beings real
Of which our dreams the ideals are.
'Balm'd in the Past, pale memory flowers
Beneath the Present's touch reblush,
And to make glad the Future's hours
There stands sweet Art, with harp and brush.
The past cannot be changed—but, dear,
How oft misread! We wait for signs,

When one deep gaze of faith would clear
   Some mystery between the lines—
         Between the lines,
         Between the lines,
         Some mystery between the lines.

COMPROMISE.

(In reverse of Jean Ingelow's " Divided.")

IT was just before the river pours into the main.
   O how we who loved stray so far apart!
Said he, " Day closeth—loose the bateau chain,
     Sail over, sail over to me, Sweetheart!"
   Said I, " The distance is not wide—
    Sail thou over to my side."
  Both were right and both were wrong—
  Both were weak and both were strong—
       As lovers are.

Behind us mourned the ocean, and before the willows
   sigh'd;
The day was closing starless, and the nightwinds
   made us shiver.
So far from home, so lonely—but the lover's staff is
   pride,
And the bateau chains remained unloosed on either
   side the river.
   Said he, " I'll wend love's way alone."
   Said I, " Love doth for love atone."
So he on his side, I on mine,
   Turned our faces tow'rd one shrine—
       Toward love's white star.

Ah! but it was dreary, dreary, walking there alone,
Walking there alone together in our foolish pride,

A passing sea-wind caught a human moan
And interwafted it from side to side.
    Feet were sore, and hearts were bursting,
    Unkist lips for kisses thirsting,
    Still the river roll'd between us,
    And our eyes still fixed on Venus
                Eastering.

Lo! dawn's milkwhite steeds are furrowing the orient
    into gold.
"Sail half way, love—I'll meet you in the middle of
    the river."
In one breath came two voices. And behold!
    Venus melting with a quiver
        From the oriental skies
        Rebeams in my lover's eyes,
    And lo! no bateau need we launch—
    Past river, rivulet, brook and branch,
             We've reach'd the spring.

FIRST GRIEF.

LEAVE her alone. She knows the flowers are
    blooming.
She's saddest when the rose blows reddest now.
Nay! weave no roseate coronet for her brow
And tell her it were regally becoming,—
She would but feel their thorn-pricks, her redooming,
Like sharp fate edicts, to unswaging woe;
Their red were but a background for her glooming.
When God's has fail'd, thy comfort were presuming'
You have not loved and lost. Leave her alone.

Leave her alone. She knows the birds are singing,
She's saddest when the birds sing maddest now.

Their passionate cadences are only bringing
Back mem'ries of a bliss she must forego—
An ear forever deaf to music's ringing,
A form beneath the myrtle bough's laid low,
A foot forever still'd from manhood's springing,
A heart forever dead to passion's swinging,—
You have not lost and loved.   Leave her alone.

Leave her alone.   She knows the sun is shining.
She's saddest when the sun shines brightest now.
Swing not faith's torch 'round grief's midnight re-
　　pining,
'Twill only stagger with its blinding glow.
Pain's furnace-fires are better for refining,
Albeit they seem to issue from below.
Leave her to-day to agony's consigning—
Leave her to weep, her myrtle garlands twining;
God knoweth when to turn the " silvery lining "—
Christ when to lift her eyes.   Leave her alone.

SONG IN ABSENCE.

O WHERE can I look for the blue of her eyes,
　　And where for the silvery light of her hair ?
I turn in vain to the sunset skies,
In vain to the blossoming meadows fair—
　　Nor hue in heaven, nor hue on lea
　　For mine absent one can comfort me.

O where can I look for the white of her hand,
And where can I go for the balm of her lips ?
I turn to the shells on the ocean strand
To the spicy winds that waft her ships—
　　Nor light that lingers on land or sea
　　For mine absent one can comfort me.
　10

O where shall I list for the chime of her voice,
And where shall I seek for the gold of her words?
Not all the bells of Paradise,
Nor all the music of all the birds,
    Nor gold of Ophir or Araby,
    Nor hue in heaven, nor hue on lea,
    Nor light that lingers on land or sea
    For mine absent friend can comfort me.

LAOMI: A DIRGE.

WILL ye tell me, O birds of the air,
    Where Laomi is gone?
Her voice was as clear as your very own,—
    As soft and as clear
As silverbells calling to vesper-prayer.
        She was fair—so fair—
           And her hair—
'Twas the color of dusk that the starlight falls on.
    Did you see her face, did you hear her tone,
In that beautiful mystical far-away haven to which
  you were flown
        When winter was here?—
      Will ye tell me, O birds of the air,
      Where Laomi is gone?

Will ye tell me, O sweet wild flowers,
    Where Laomi is gone?
Her breath was as sweet as your very own,
And her heart was as deep and as golden as yours.
    Has she wandered off, apart and alone,
      To one of your bowers,
        There amidst showers
  Of sweet-scented petals to lay her down,
To be charmëd and chain'd by the golden hours,

And circled away to that magical island that knoweth no moan?
                    Will ye tell me, O sweet wild flowers,
                        Where Laomi is gone?

Will ye tell me, O breezes of even,
      Where Laomi is gone?
Her sigh was as sad as your very own,
      When Anemone-riven
      You were, and outdriven
And banished by Flora her queen, jealous grown,
Have you seen Laomi—or heard her moan?
                    Have you woo'd her and shriven
                    Her sorrow and given
Her wings to float off, like your eiderdown,
Over treetop and hilltop and into the faraway azure
  of heaven?
                    Will ye tell me, O breezes of even,
                        Where Laomi is gone?

Will ye tell me, O stars of the night,
      Where Laomi is gone?
Her eyes were as bright as your very own,
      As soft and as bright;
      And her hands were as white,
      As tapering and white,   [height
As the wings of the saints that descend Heaven's
                    When twilight is flown.
      Have ye envied her eyes' pure topazolite,
      And over their lids an influence thrown,
That a new Gemini, outrivalling the old, in the
  heavens be sown?
                    Will ye tell me, O stars of the night,
                        Where Laomi is gone?

Will ye tell me, O silver-sail'd ships,
    Where Laomi is gone?
Her glide was as graceful as your very own,
As she passed from my presence to pastures unknown.
      Did her sea-shell ears and her coral lips
      Old ocean's gems so far eclipse
That he snatched her hence?—Is she now floating on
His beautiful breast as it rises and dips?
Or have the mermaidens allur'd her down to their
   submarine crypts

           To sit on a coraline throne?
      Will ye tell me, O silver-sail'd ships,
          Where Laomi is gone?
Wilt thou tell me, O Heaven (God knoweth),
    Where Laomi is gone?
Her soul was as white as the soul of your own
Saints who have passed from the cross to the crown.
        As a flower that bloweth
        Man cometh and goeth;
      To-day he is sown,
      To-morrow cut down,
And even the place thereof is unknown.
Was she needed above?   Hath an angel downflown
To uplift, lest her foot be dashed on a stone,
And bear her away to that river that floweth,
      Floweth by God's White Throne—
         On and on—
On to a blissful endless end where no boat roweth—
    Wilt thou tell me, O Heaven (God knoweth),
      Where Laomi is gone?

THOU ART TO ME.

(Set to music by Signor Aldo Guiseppe Randegger.)

THOU art to me a light—
   But for thy guiding ray
My pilgrim feet would stray
Away from right.

Thou art to me a balm,
An incense-lamp for Art,
Burning upon my heart
Steady and calm.

Thou art to me a prayer—
A living orison,
Mounting each day upon
Heaven's unseen stair.

Thou art to me a voice—
Of all earth's cadences
Tuned to the softest keys;
A poet's choice.

Thou art to me—And I ?—
Love doth for love atone.
Ah ! leave me not alone
In this cold world to die.

Be what thou art to me—
My light, my balm, my voice.
Heaven would not be my choice
Except with thee.

AT MOUNT ENOTA'S LAUREL'D BASE.

AT Mount Enota's laurel'd base,
  Where Hiawassee's waters flash,
'Twas there I met a mountain grace,
  Beautiful Ida Ash.

As o'er the rocks, nereidianly,
  She moved, with lissom step and proud,
Her eyes gleam'd like the Gemini
  Beneath a shifting summer cloud.

The east-wind left its mourning cave
  To nestle, dove-like, in her locks;
Tamed by her step, each madcap wave
  Caress'd the conscious rocks.

The skylarks left their aëry thrones
  Amidst the serenading stars,
To catch her accent's Orphean tones
  And beat its elegiac bars.

"*Ah, I have sigh'd to rest me,*" sang
  She from *Il Trovatore;* and thro'
A poet's heart the echo rang,
  "*Ah, I have sigh'd to rest me, too.*"

Sweet Ida Ash! life's hills are steep,
  And Art a glad toil at its best;
Then rest thou in my heart, and I
  Sweetly in thine will rest.

Teach me to sing as thou dost live,
  A simple life of love and duty;
Then I at least to Art may give
  One song of everlasting beauty.

SONNETS.

SONNETS.

A. TEAR.

A CHEMIST took a human tear and made
   A nice analysis thereof. Saline,
So many parts; with hydro-oxygen
Admix'd, so much. To a drop of water add
A grain of salt—and there the tear you had—
Of little worth—in fact, 'twas useless, when
The ocean teem'd therewith. A poet then,
Who listening stood, and knew it had been shed—
This tear—by a mother, did thus analyze
It silently. Of joy, so many parts;
With travail, patience, and self-sacrifice
Admix'd so much. Take a heartful of bliss—
Stir in experience—and there it is.
Its worth? The fountain whence faith's ocean starts.

PRETTY-BY-NIGHTS.

EVEN as a child I had my favorites
   Among the flowers. Most children have, I think.
Some take to buttercups; to some the pink
Is most adorable. My pet delights
Were, violets first, and then—the pretty-by-nights!
How blissfully at twilight would I sink
In the cool grass, with wimpleful, and link
Chain after chain of yellows, reds and whites—

And, O ! the variegated—did they grow
Once in the skies ?—I made so many guesses—
Maybe God dropt them o'er the rainbow's rim.
All on a separate charmstring they must go,
To ring into a rainbow-crown for him
Who soon would meet me at the gate with kisses.

A LITTLE BOY.

A LITTLE boy I know, so bright of face,
    So dimpled-sweet, so bubbling o'er with mirth,
He seems a brooklet gushing from the earth,
And gurgling softly now o'er pebbly place,
And bounding now o'er tiny precipice.
Please God, may he yet be some noble firth,
And wash to shore the pearls of goodliest worth
That undiscover'd lie at ocean's base—
Some strong arm of the sea, where argosies
Of lofty purposes may safely steer
Their freight to God's eternal ocean-pier.
Bound on, brave little brook ! so blithe, so merry—
Gain strength for burdens here, and beyond the skies
Be of the River of Life a tributary.

A LITTLE MAID.

A LITTLE maid I know, so dainty-fair,
    So cunning-arch, so sunning o'er with sweets,
Who when her "Nama" comes, with kisses greets
Her on her hands and on her silver hair,
And leads her laughing to an easy-chair,
Then in her lap her fairy form she seats,
And holds her close, so close their two heart-beats

Seem doubled one.   And gazing on them there,
Love-lockt, and all unconscious of my bliss,
Love-lockt, love-loos'd, and bartering kiss for kiss,
Youth's gold with wisdom's silver intermixt—
I stand as one enraptur'd and transfixt,
So part of very heaven seems the scene.
If angels visit earth, 'tis here, I ween.

LIFE'S PARADOX.

THEY are the happiest who know most pain.
    In even the saddest life to every tear
A thousand smiles are shed.   Our rainiest year
Has more of sunshine in it than of rain.
Joy's golden ring o'ermeasures Sorrow's train.
Ah ! point me out that form which o'er the bier
Has longest lingered, shaking in sincere
Exuberancy of grief—has oftest lain
Upon a noonday couch in ecstasy
Of midnight wretchedness—and I will say,
There lies the heart that beats the quickest time
'Neath Love's soft finger-touch.   Capacity
For suffering is but that for joying.   They
Who sound woe's depths, the heights of rapture climb.

GRANDMOTHER'S GARDEN.

I.

GRANDMOTHER'S garden was the sweetest spot
    Ever I walk'd in on a summer's day !
Sweeter than violets, or new-mown hay,
Sweeter than Eden asphodels, I wot.
If all the Oriental zephyrs brought

Their spicy stores from blessed Araby
And pour'd them at my feet, I would turn away
If from Grandmother's garden I but caught
One faintest whiff. And then, that clean white walk—
Swept every morn, or e'er she wander'd down it,
With her pet flowers to have a sunrise talk;
Those blackberry-rows and raspberry-rows, so trim;
The sage, coriander, mint, and sweet wild-thyme—
Grandmother's garden was a perfect sonnet!

II.

THE *double-quatrain* was, eight rows of corn,
   Iam'd with reds and yellows, blues and greens
Of lesser vegetables, by which means
One pass'd thro' unsprinkl'd on a dewy morn;
Hollyhocks, ruby and golden, did adorn
The alternate ends with rhymes, to which a queen's
Ear might have paus'd to listen—or a dean's
Fresh from an Easter choral.   Not a thorn
Or thistle dared discordant foot to set
Amidst the harmony of that *sextette.*
Amethyst mad-apples, chrysoprasus pears,
Emerald asparagus, beryl Delawares—
Sweet as the manna that came down to Moses—
And that last rainbow line of diamond roses!

III.

GRANDMOTHER'S bonnet was inviolate white—
   White like her robe, her hair—white like her soul:
Against it the Bride roses' white was dull,
And the Pearl roses, yellow as chrysolite;

"La France's" cameo, a peach-blow bright;
The "Sunset's" amber pink, a beautiful
Deep after-glow; and when she stoop'd to cull
A "Jacqueminot" the acme was reached quite
Of perfect contrast: black were more at home
Against her sorrowing white than red or yellow.
But, ah! the background that did most become
Grandmother in her garden, were the hues
That fell iridescent from the "Rainbow" rose—
All that her pure brow lack'd was just that halo.

IV.

GRANDMOTHER'S garden was so generous.
Brides got their bouquets there, and altar-bells;
Sickbeds, their cheer and solace; funerals,
Their wreaths and anchors. Lovers might discuss
Within its bowers their plans felicitous,
And dainty children thro' its fairy dells
Ramble and pick their choice of asphodels
And berries. And with what magnanimous
Right hand were heap'd its baskets for the poor,
The left hand all-unknowing; with what grace
It kept supplied the sacred fireside vase,
Each morning with fresh frankincense and myrrh;
And with what golden pride and purple state
It crown'd the honor'd guest within the gate!

LEIGH HUNT, MY BIRD.
I.

I CALL my bird Leigh Hunt, because he sings
　　So cheerfully in prison.　It is meet
That Poesy, to bear out the conceit,
Give him a garden ; so I stick green things
About him boweringly.　See how he swings
On yonder mimic bush, his pink-ribb'd feet
Quivering beneath him with sensation sweet
Of new-found freedom, and his dainty wings
(Lo, how he spreads them fan-like in the sun!)
Seem like a patch of silken moonlight spun.
Leigh Hunt, my Bird! look not beyond the stars,
And pine to skim with larks the aerial blue.
Leigh Hunt, the Poet, made his prison-bars
A Paradise : and so will I make yours for you.

II.

LEIGH HUNT, my Bird, he hath a sunny soul,
　　And prone, I think, by nature, to content.
What tho' the Destinies have cruelly pent
Him thus within a little gilded hole?—
Shall he for this espouse his tongue to dole,
And all his melody in wails be spent?
Yet sometimes I misdoubt this glad ostent
His heart is breaking, and mine own is full
With fellow-feeling ; sometimes he grows sad
And hangs his head, and when I say, "Sing sweet!"
Draws only from his breast a low "*tu-weet.*"
Leigh Hunt, my Bird! Leigh Hunt, the Poet, had
His love in prison with him.　That is why
He never lonesome grew, as you and I.

MY SHAKESPEARE.

MY Shakespeare.   Golden privilege, thus to thy
     Death-daring name the symbol to prefix
Of my possessing.   Doth the coupling vex,
Seeming irreverent, thy memory?
Nay, thou art mine.   When God the world had brought
Thro' her sixth labor, perfect in all parts,
He sent thee down—celestial after-thought—
To gather up and save His children's hearts.
And thou didst pick them up and 'twixt the pages
Of an immortal tome as relics press,
Where they will linger thro' the unnumber'd ages,
To draw man's laughter, wonder, and distress.
And, great Heart-Gatherer! so sublime thine art
Thou reach'd'st out o'er the years and caught'st my
     heart.

WORDSWORTH.

A SIMPLE man; who lov'd life's quiet ways,
     Who found a friend in every flower and bird,
And in each passing breeze a music heard,
To weave in song-chains for his linkèd days.
A sensuous man; whom every varying phase
Of nature with a sacred import stirr'd;
Yet nothing pantheistic in his word—
To one revealèd God is all the praise.
A passionate man; who yet in calm control
Held every deep emotion of the soul:
His tears his wisdom never overran—
We feel, not see, the emotion running thro' it.
Wordsworth—a simple, sensuous, passionate man—
An ideal type—a very Milton's poet.

MRS. BROWNING.

FIRST woman singer.   Strongest of the weak,
   Weakest in body of the strong in soul ;
Whose genius, flashing 'thwart, from pole to pole,
The firmament of poesy, left a streak
Of light will shed its influence whilst we speak
"The tongue which Shakespeare spake."   If o'er the
Where geniuses their honor'd names enroll,   [scroll
When they have climb'd fame's utmost mountain-peak,
I were permit to pass mine eye and choose
A name to leave behind me when I die,
Elizabeth Barrett Browning would it be—
For aye God-dedicated to the Muse.
But if her spotless path my feet might lead,
I'd ask of Fame no crowning laurel meed.

BROWNING.

I MUST confess a preference for *her*.
   The purest sparks he left us, to my thought,
Are those fine dartling reds and blues he caught
From her who was professedly his star.
Howbeit, so esteeming, I would not debar
His lofty memory of one tiniest jot
Of deep-earn'd homage.   If his muse had wrought
No other miracle than the rhythmic snare
Wherein was meshed that woman's vestal heart,
She would have mark'd herself a master muse.
But should the poet play logician's part
And poet's too?   I can but wish, *sometimes*,
He had winnow'd out the logic from his rhymes—
Or the rhymes from his logic, as you choose.

TENNYSON AND LONGFELLOW.

IF poets, like disciples, go in pairs,
    Then is my pair well-sorted—Tennyson
And Longfellow. In what sweet unison
Their spirits soared !—what mutual smiles and tears
They shed, thro' all those serenading years
The Atlantic roll'd between them. When the crown
Of England paus'd to lay on brow of one
The wreath of peerage, she, not unawares,
Did honor to that ever-during name,
Victoria. It were Columbia's shame
Had she, being like invested, left unlaid
Like wreath on the other's brow. Peer him she did—
With love. To-day beneath the Stars and Stripes
The Psalm of Life sounds on a million lips.

GRAY.

THEY came across a faded manuscript
    Of Gray's—time-yellow'd, crumpled, mildewpied—
Husk that the Elegy had cast aside
When forth it fruited perfect. Here was clipt
The fungus sentiment, and there outslipt
The phrase ambiguous ; here fortified
The tottering idea, and there applied
Art's emery till Promethean lustre leapt
From hackney'd gem of thought : so interlined,
So marginalia-strewn, 'twere hard to find
Where lapsed the lucid theme. Less priz'd therefore ?
Nay, rather priz'd an hundredfold the more.
Ne'er yet Pierian font gusht crystal forth
That had not toil'd thro' rock-beds under earth.

II

LANIER.

MUSIC and Poesy, by some sweet chance,
　　Met in the Valley of Humiliation.
Folded their wings were ; in deep meditation
Each hung a head, and made slow advance.
Never a motion made they for a dance—
Never a hint to enter conversation ;
Only a low, scarce-utter'd lamentation,
Each gazing sad in other's countenance.
Music was searching for a word—alas,
So long had been the quest ; and Poesy
Was searching for a sound.　A tear—
A mutual tear—upon the fragrant grass
They dropt, and kist, and parted.　Presently
Upsprung a pure-white asphodel—Lanier.

"AFTER SORROW'S NIGHT."

NOT many birds have made homes in the trees
　　That border my song-garden.　Many light,
And flute a fancy, or a berry bite,
Then wing them otherwhere on some soft breeze
That beckons.　Haply 'tis the cypresses
Whose gloom lets in too scantily heaven's bright,
Or else the weeping willows, that invite
Not serenaders—or the draperies
Of moss that veil my roses from the blight
Of southern sun.　Ah, but nathless there are
Some rare sweet song-birds here,—some from afar,
Over the centuries and the seas, have flown ;
Others from climes Columbian—of these, one—
Gilder—most soothes me after Sorrow's night.

COWPER'S MARY.

I THOUGHT once of the women who had been
   The beacon-lights of bards—whose influent ray
For years had guided them, by night and day,
Safe 'round the glittering vortices of sin,
And thro' the eclipses of bereavement, when
The spirit travaileth : in whose constancy
Their souls, being pois'd, had mounted patiently
And surely upward into heaven's serene.
So retrospecting, rose the visions fair
Of that immortal lady Florentine—
Of Dante's Beatrice Portinari,
Who enter'd him into the life divine ;
And Petrarch's Laura, with her eyes of prayer ;
And—gentlest, tenderest, truest – Cowper's Mary.

MILTON'S DAUGHTERS.

IF ours such bliss is at this distance wide
   Communing with thee, Milton, how tenfold
The joy of those two who did sit and hold
Thy blind hands pulsing ; or did eager guide
Them to thy sacred harp, not unallied
To harps angelic, when with visions bold
Thy spirit burst its earth-bands, and out-roll'd
In golden fullness floodtide on floodtide
Of melody majestic ; or did dive
With thee antiquity's dim ocean-caves
For sacred pearls, or mythologic coral ;
Or did, with womanly and sensitive
Fingers, enwreathe thy tresses' silvery waves,
Over thy sightless brows, with redolent laurel.

EMMA HAHR.

A MIRACLE.   A veiled rhapsody.
What angel left the gates of Heaven ajar
That thro' the portal there should waft a bar
Of the great Symphony of the To-Be?
A wingèd measure of divinity—
Fallen in our midst in veil of Emma Hahr.
Earth leaps towards Heaven, her elements at war:
See horrid Clamor skulk—Discordancy
Creep to his lair—Mirth swoon into her grave—
All nature throbs—the sweet-voiced birds are shy—
The shell withholds its message from the wave—
The winds go whispering, " A mystery ! "—
Whilst old Pythagoras from his distant sphere
Leans worldward with his star-attunèd ear.

WASHINGTON.

NOT to our Country's father, deep-rever'd,
Nor to her Capital of wide renown,
But to a modest little Georgia town,
My monumental sonnet is now reared.
An Eden: here the most fastidious bird
Of Paradise might find a nest of down.
An Arcadie: here Hesper might have sown
The Garden of Hesperides, where star'd
The apples of pure gold upon the trees ;
But here need not have labored Hercules
To slay the guarding dragon.   Air so pure
No fiend could breathe an hour, and endure ;
Nor Greed's own self could cast a covetous eye
On this fair bower of Generosity.

A GEORGIA GLOAMING.

AUTUMN. That hour of grace when moon and sun
    Each full in other's face serenely gaze
Across a charmèd world. 'Twere vain to trace
The lines where sunlights into moonlights run,
So subtle is the interfusion
Of gold and silver, gentle greens and grays,
And dying rose. A silken filmy lace
Of white diaphanous cloud, Arachne-spun,
Is portier'd o'er th' horizon's western gate:
One white-torch'd vestal enters ; others wait,
Timid, till Dian sweep the curtains wide,
Upon a variegated hillock-side.
Under the serenading pines, I roam,
And in this pilgrim world feel strangely at home.

A FLORIDA AFTERGLOW.

OVER against a gloom of cypresses,
    A long cold stratum of pale saffron sheen ;
O'er this, thin layers of sapphire and aquamarine—
Now melting to a tender opal haze—
Now dulling to a morbid chrysoprase—
Now bright'ning to a sanguine emerald green—
Now soft'ning to an amethyst serene—
Now deepening to an ominous topaz—
Now firing to a passionate ruby red,
Which o'er the heav'ns doth instantly outspread,
As naval battle-blood spilt on the seas
Incarnadines the ambient waves.   Now white
Hesper advanceth, with th' Hesperides,
And, without twilight courtesy, 'tis night.
    Lake Minnehaha.

CHRISTMAS AT LOCH KATRINE.

NOT Scottish Loch Katrine, but Loch Katrine
  In Flora-land. A thousand Christmas trees,
Swing golden bounty to the bounding breeze,
Till the white sand is dotted with the green
And red and yellow of lime, tangerine,
And orange. (With their hoarded treasuries,
Grape-fruit and shaddock groan : One sometimes
  sees
The groaning rich so hoard their wealth, which, when
Thieves break thro' and steal it, proves a bitter-
  sweet.)
With all this generous outlay at my feet ;
With all that gives the senses pleasant taste,
And feeds the heart—friends, books, birds, flowers
  galore,—
The thought comes o'er me of the northern poor,
To whom what God-send were this lavish waste !

YALAHA–ON–ASTATULA.

YALAHA-ON-ASTATULA—interpreted,
  "Sweet Orange on the Lake of Sunbeams."
    How
Those Indian names out-music ours ! I trow
Some ichor mingles with the warlike red
In their barbarian veins. Pan might have led
His shepherds forth to such a spot. And O !
What choice of reeds he had found here to blow ;
And how his bees had suck'd yon lotus-bed,
And in these wild magnolias held grand court,

Or, cloyed with revelry, had restful swung
On yonder flaming vine of Devil's Tongue,
Or drows'd on Spanish Bayonet's bright edge ;
And just beyond that marge of lush green sedge,
His fishermen had found what royal sport !

"ONCE IN MIDWINTER WOODS IN FLORA-LAND."

ONCE in midwinter woods in Flora-land
    I found a violet hiding 'neath a heart.
Dear modest thing ! I said, how like thou art
To one I know, and hold in reverend
Affection—one who her sweet life doth spend
In calm retiracy—doth dwell apart,
Like Wordsworth's Lucy. Yet—as thee—the alert
Poet is quick to espy her and to band
The globe with her encomiums—aye ! since
The modest wield the largest influence.
If every pillow that upholds my faith
Were swept to earth in one wild tide of doubt,
Still would the fragrance of her life creep out
Amidst the ruins and rescue me from death.

"AS DAY BY DAY I SEEK SOME SYLVAN ISLE."

AS day by day I seek some sylvan isle,
    More solitary than the one before,
To sonnet my Belovèd, angels oar
My shallop for me, and I seem the while
To be alone in heaven, with heaven's smile

Beaming soft sanction down, what time I pour
My heart out at the feet of one I adore
With tender reverence.　Rhyming so, I toil
Not, for the vesper zephyrs plash serene
Amongst the water-lilies and the sedge
Lilteth a measure for my thoughts, that pledge,
And swing, and tilt, and nothing hindereth,
Like golden goblets on the jasmine-vine—
Just pouring out the bliss God fill'd them with.

GRACE.

THAT influent subtlety, intangible,
　　Which charms, we know not why, we care not
　　　　how.
Saints condescend before it, monarchs bow,
And poets (Heaven help us) prostrate fall,
O'ercome at unawares—aye, give up all
Besides for it, and count loss gain, if so
We may but blissful hover to and fro
About it, and may feel the rhythmical
Wave of its breath, or touch the fragrant hem
Of its white garment : even on the ground
Whence it hath vanish'd will we sit and twine
Sad garlands, rather than with diadem
Of glittering gold and diamonds be crown'd,
Or bend the knee at any other shrine.

HER EYES.

ADOWN into the depths of thy true eyes
   One only needs to look to trust in thee,
For there dwell sadness and sincerity,
Just as they followed Eve from Paradise.
If e'er and anon upon their surface lies
Mirth, in a semblance-garb of sovereignty,
She glisters there a moment bubblingly,
Then glints away in laughterful surprise,
Seeing she did mistake her proper sphere.
And so with Coquetry and Pride and Scorn—
They can but scintillate with transient flashes
From 'neath those lids—Ah ! nothing as a tear
(Albeit thy life hath not yet spent its morn)
Is so becoming to those drooping lashes.

HER HAND.

A SONNET to her hand.   My harpsichord,
   Had I but such an one to sweep thy keys,
Then might I set about, less ill at ease,
A task which, to my fingers, seems absurd
As painting Shakespeare's lily.   Harp ne'er stirr'd
To such a hopeless cadence.   Bossy frieze
Beneath the chisel of Praxiteles
Show'd not such cunning curves.   There is no word
Save snow to call its whiteness by—and snow
Forsooth, is pulseless, cold.   Till thou, like me,
Had'st felt its palpitant warmth, thou would'st not
How poor this best comparison would be.   [know
Her hand—too white and tender to emboss,
But not too tender-white to bear a cross.

"SINCE OUR SOULS CROSSED."

SINCE our souls crossed, sweet soul, my soul hath
  In the Eternal Now,—no *might have been*, [dwelt
No *was*, no *will be*, but the great serene
It is—Light is, Life is, Love is : I felt
It at the moment at thy side I knelt,
And when I awak'd and gaz'd around, 'twas seen—
God's kingdom in this beauteous land terrene,—
Not in one chosen spot, one narrow belt,
But outstretch'd o'er the world—which is not sad,
Which is not hopeless, is not woe-predoom'd,
But by the fire of faith updrawn, consumed
Into Truth's sun, upleapeth and is glad.
It is—Light is, Life is, Love is—and even
Now dwell we in the kingdom of His Heaven.

A SONG TO COOL MY LADY.

A SONG to cool my lady.   Let it be
  All made of breezes, shades, and fountain spray—
A flower or two—white flowers—roses, say—
Pale climbing roses, of faint fragancy
And broad green leaves ; a gentle melody—
Barili's Cradle Song, or two or three
Measures from Schubert's Serenade in E ;
A passage from Longfellow's Rainy Day ;
Sidney Lanier's Last Sigh ; a revery
Of sails upon the soul's Vesuvius Bay ;
A night-wind rustling thro' a myrtle tree ;
A silver glimpse into futurity ;
A veil of cameo o'er an emerald sea ;
Shadows of snow-clouds on a moonlit lea.

SLEEP. I.

AT midnight Sleep, the mocker, came to me—
My best friend turn'd to foe !—and o'er my bed
Dallied his poppied wand, but took a heed
Lest it should touch mine eyelids—I could see
It hovering there like the apple on the tree   [said,
When Tantalus reach'd in vain.   " Sweet friend," I
" Draw nearer—touch me with thy charmèd reed—
Sprinkle mine eyes with lotus *pot-pourri*—
Mine aching temples cool with Lethe-spray—
Let but thy soporific finger-tips
O'er pass my brow—or thy mesmeric lips
Breathe on my pillow."—"Nay! my sweet one, nay !"
(As out into the shimmering night he flies)
" Bid *Poesy* kiss to thy wakeful eyes."

SLEEP. II.

AT daydawn Sleep, relenting, came to me—
My old, old comrade Sleep, came as of old—
Came gliding swiftly o'er my glad threshold,
Whose door had known his tread and turn'd the key
Of welcome—came, and O, so tenderly
Did kiss mine eyelids down, and warm my cold
Hands 'twixt his pulsing own, and close enfold
Me in his downy arms.   O Araby
The Blest! thou hast no balm like this !
No sails like this down the Vesuvius Bay !
No bed of autumn leaves so soft, I wis,
In Valambrosian vales—as when sweet sleep
In golden odors did my senses steep
And bring me rest that morn—and dreams of thee !

"IN EVERY HEART SOME NOBLE NERVES THERE ARE."

IN every heart some noble nerves there are,
  Which touch'd upon by jest recoil with shock.
'Twixt ridicule, that only lives to mock,
And that pure laugh that cheers—what gulf is there !
If from my soul arises one deep prayer
Unceasingly, it is that God may lock
The gate-ways of mine ears to all who knock
There with unbrotherly messages, and bar
The portal of my lips from letting out
Those imps of ridicule and ghouls of doubt
That will at times in every breast arise.
God-fus'd in us, as colors in the flowers,
Our feelings are our own—*all* that are ours—
Which only God, and time, can alchemize.

TO SONNET-BUILDERS : A MESSAGE.

I OWE you apology for thus venturing.
  Allegiance drives me to it, and pure love
Of Art, my queen.   Certes it doth behoove
Me, her most loyal handmaiden, to bring
A message to her subjects.   Murmuring
Is not my gift : if I malfeasance prove,
'Tis only at the instigation of
Her whom I serve.   It is a simple thing,
This message I now read, by her command,
To sonnet-builders :—*Start not in the skies*
To build your stately mansions, Chinese-wise,
Down-rushing headlong to a bed of sand ;
But lay you first a wise foundation down,
Then lift your polish'd columns one by one.

THE PIERIDES.

CLIO, MELPONENE AND CALLIOPE.

IN dreams thro' Tempe's vale I took my stroll,
  And met the Pierides—in groups of three
And two. First Clio, muse of History,
Holding her cithara and half-open'd scroll :
Close at her right, with mask, and parchment roll,
And club of Hercules, was Melpomene,
Vine-wreath'd and buskin-shod for tragedy ;
Whiles on her left arm lean'd the beautiful
Mother of Orpheus, Calliope—queen
Of Homer's soul—with epic pen,
And close-roll'd tablet. Charmèd-wise,
I gaz'd on this great classic trinity.
But when each held a goddess hand to me
For tribute—wavering, I let fall mine eyes.

QUEEN SOUTH.

WHEN our fair South was young and olden-new,
  Her sunny curls by passion yet unshorn,
To her red lips she laid the sounding horn,
And to her banquets all the nations flew,
And all the four winds of the heavens blew
Praise of her purple bounty. Alas, one morn

She fell, our queen.   A brother king, twin-born,
Question'd her right-of-way, challeng'd her, drew
From her unyielding waist the key of keys
Wherewith she unlock'd her treasure.   There were
    left
Others upon her girdle, and with these,
Fitting them here and there, with fingers deft,
Tho' bleeding still, she pass'd from door to door,
And oped new vaults of wealth undream'd before.

ATLANTA.

FIRST Lady of the South!   Thy diamond eyes
    Full many a suitor lure, as did of old
Fair Atalanta's—but, as hers, still hold
Them at proud distance, till one win the prize
In conquering foot-race.   Prithee now, be wise—
Be circumspect, sweet maiden! lest some bold
Foreign Hippomenes, with apple of gold
Roll'd off the track, thy charmèd eye entice,
And so win first the goal, and claim thy lips—
Rightfully ours, who hew'd thy woods primeval,
Thy virgin valleys fill'd, and hills made level—
And now thine international gates unlock.
Give royal entrance unto all who knock—
But save thy kisses for the Stars and Stripes.

EDISON.

LATE, led by Edison, I stood upon
    The Mount of Progress—in its western wing—
And there did hap so passing strange a thing
As doth, meseems, deserve the setting down.

Before me pass'd three figures, one by one.
First, a boy cherub, who did dance and sing,
Disporting in a wise so rollicking,
"Certes," cried I, "that's Cupid!" Edison
Said, "Nay, that's *Time*." Next, hobbling, came
A dwarf, so shrunk of form, so pinch'd of face.
"That's Death!" I shudder'd. "Nay," said he,
    "that's *Space*."
An angel, last, with robes so dazzling-white,
"Ah!" burst I forth, "no need that vision name—
That's Life." "Nay," answer'd Edison, "that's
    Night."

A STORM.

MID-SEA. A million stars. The vessel's name
    Is Harmony; the Captain, Equipoise;
The crew, Endurance, Silence, Faith, and Joy's
Twin daughters, Peace and Laughter. Thro' the
    gleam
Of Milky Way downdarts a blue-edged flame
Of forkèd fury, follow'd by a noise
Of thunder-wheels. Old Ocean in a trice
Accepts the challenge, and upspouts a stream
That outs the stars. Now horrid war prevails,
And Chaos revels. Equipoise o'erboard,
Tottering, falls; Peace brandishes a sword;
Endurance swoons away; and Laughter wails;
While Faith, blaspheming, turns to Infidel,
And Silence lifts a shriek that startles hell.

A CALM.

DAWN. Not a star. The birds still think it night.
　　The insects, subtler, feeling day's approach,
Have still'd their tiny harps. I feel the touch
Of something on my cheek: it is the white
Lake-mist arising, like an acolyte
For matin mass, or ere the world encroach
On holy hour. Now from her silver coach,
Drawn by grey steeds in sober livery dight,
Sad-eyed Aurora peers, as in a dream,
The reins fall'n from her hands. In this pale beam,
I see a mesh of thistledown at poise
In mid-air, motionless. I hear a noise.
I turn : a dewdrop from the o'erhanging brake
Hath plasht upon the surface of the lake.

COMPOSURE.

A LURID battle-plain – the crucial pitch
　　Of arms betwixt two nations match'd to a man.
A circling cloud, brewing a hurricane,
With mutterings weird as those of Macbeth's witch—
Now with Cyclopian oaths and shrieks eldritch
Its seething pot upsetting on the plain,
That liquid choler flows thro' rear and van
And o'er the slaughter'd loved ones in the ditch.
Behold, whiles earth and skies are warring thus,
Like feudal ranks of the Satanic band,
Within the crater of Vesuvius,
Her first-born clinging to her milkless breast,
A mother refugee lies down to rest,
As in the hollow of the Almighty hand.

POLYHYMNIA AND URANIA.

THE twain that greeted now my lifted eyes
Were Polyhymnia and Urania. Fair
Indeed they were: one held a lyre of rare
Exquisite workmanship—the pure device
Of her own genius—which in pensive wise
She brush'd, and raised her azure eyes in prayer—
First of all mundane goddesses to dare
Approach the most high gods with melodies;
The other in her right hand held a sphere
Celestial, pointing to it with her left,
As if to indicate the god to whom
Her sister paid her adoration. There
I paused enraptured, and my hand was swift
To lay at feet of each a laurel bloom.

HESPER.

AMBITIOUS orb! thou usherest in the night
E'en ere the golden dust by Phœbus' train
Rais'd in the west hath settled in the main;
E'en ere Diana's self dare claim her right
Of way into her special realm, thy white
Incense-breathing lantern thou art fain
To swing out in the heavens. Charles' Wain
Is not so aspiring; nor the diamond-bright
Orion; nor Aldebaran, flaming eye
Of Taurus; nor the yokèd Gemini;
Nor Cassiopeia's Chair illuminous;
Nor Sickle's glittering curve; nor Sirius,
With his swift-scorching scintillations;
Nor Milky Way, with its quintillion suns.

THE OPAL.

ON wings of special lightning Jove has sent
    Iris to Tempe's vale, where stroll the Nine.
News is arriving at the Delphian shrine,
Upon the posting east, of deep moment
And dreaded sequence.   In the Orient
A bright star would arise, that self-same e'en,
Of such transcendent lustre as to outshine
The Olympian volts combin'd ; by whose portent
He might be warn'd, an angel's song would rise
Of such glad tidings the Pierides   [wonder
Would thenceforth lack a theme.   Which when in
The weeping Sisters hear, with ne'er a scruple
They hang their sorrowing harps on the oleander,
While Iris drops a tear that turns to an opal.

ERATO AND EUTERPE.

WHILES yet I stood, with head bow'd reverently,
    A sound so dulcet-pure crept on mine ear,
So enticing-soft, so paradisian-rare,
So insinuating-sweet, I turned—to see
Those fair twin daughters of Mnemosyne
And Zeus—for such in sooth I knew they were—
Euterpe and Erato, tender pair !
Methought of Horace and his Lalage—
And all true poets and true lovers since,
Who have paid homage to their innocence
And grace, both in and out of books.
I tarried not to do mine humble part—
Which was to shower their hyacinthine locks
With handfuls of rose-petals from my heart.

LOVE.

SOME heart-flowers, like some earthly blossoms, are
  Too chaste for human touch to dwell upon—
Too modest to unfold beneath the sun;
As the night-blooming Cereus from the glare
Of bold-eyed day conceals its charms with care—
Close-hooded, like the consecrated nun—
But bares them to the adoration
Of some fine distant deferential star—
Aye, freely unfolds its heart, in one full hour
Of lavish grace, of golden confidence—
Under the delicate heavenly influence—
E'en tho' death be the cost, such trust to prove—
Or separation, sadder: such an heart-flower,
So lavish, yet so modest-chaste is love.

ROSETIME IN WASHINGTON. (AN IDYL.)

ROSETIME in Washington. An eastern sweep
  Of cool verandah, vined with Mareschal Niels
And trailing Brides, whereover trickling steals
The sweet south, violet-laden. Thro' the deep
Green gloom of the magnolia branches, seep
The nectar'd moondrops down, and flow in rills
Of liquid gold around the lily-hills
And down the violet-borders. In their sleep,
Like slumbering babes, the breeze-rockt lilies smile,
And dream Aurora kisses them; what while
The wide-eyed jasmine-starlings glint and dance,
And dart their Cupid-arrows thither and yon,
And, percht on blushing bough of sweet La France,
The mocking-bird makes love to Lady Moon.

ANTICIPATION.

A STARLIT lawn, with hints of soft florescence.
    Alone she listeth at the lattice-height.
Of perfect days to be and full delight
Comes from rose-thicket a melodious prescience.
Not present yet, a swift-advancing Presence
Dilates the air with breathings exquisite.
That *being about to be!* how perfect, quite
O'er and beyond the being's very essence.
How sweeter than all joy is that fleet hour
That bringeth joy!   How rarer than all bliss
Is faith's deep thrill before the trothal kiss!
O! for some psychic trick, some secret power,
To pulse that moment thro' Eternity!—
That thrice supreme—that *being about to be!*

SHE HELD LIFE'S DULCIMER.

SHE held life's dulcimer, and carelessly
    Brushed o'er its diapason.   Hope and Fear,
Sorrow and Joy, Ambition and Despair—
Unto each vital chord, each fateful key,
Her heart, with more or less of sympathy,
Responded.   But 'twas not till unaware
Upon Love's golden string she dropt a tear,
There came a breath of such pure melody,
Her heart leapt up within her, all awake
And quivering with a sacred bliss—Ah, take
The harp away—it is enough, I said—
The keynote struck, the destiny is read.
Then knew I, up the angel-guarded road
Of loving one her days would link tow'rd God.

"AND EVERY MORNING AS I PASSED HER BOWER."

AND every morning as I pass'd her bower,
  I heard her singing to that tender key ;
I love you, love you, love you—thus sang she-
I love you, love you, love you—till a shower
Of golden love notes sprinkled all the floor,
And spray'd the air, that liquid cadency
Seep'd thro' the casement to the birds and me,
Who upleaning drank, and drinking upleaned more.
I love you, love you, love you—thus she sang ;
And sometimes thro' her ecstasy there rang
A minor undercadence, sweetly-sad,
As if a silver thread of sorrowing
Already mingled with love's golden string;
And other times her note was purely glad.

"HAVE YOU A RIGHT," AT FIRST SHE ASK'D HER HEART.

"HAVE you a right," at first she ask'd her heart,
  "To this great happiness that love bestoweth?"
And soft a voice made answer, "God He knoweth
When and to whom His blessings to impart.
Treasure the golden largesse. If thou art
Unworthy of such bounty, it but showeth
How his omnifluent mercy overfloweth
The meagre measure of thy life's desert."
And so she locked the God-gift in her soul,
And said, "I will live nearer to my God—
So near as lieth in a human's might;

With noble thoughts and deeds I shall extol
My spirit till it cleave its mortal clod—
And doubt not if my rapture be my right."

"I LOVE YOU SO."

" I LOVE you so, mine every thought is sweet,"
      She sang, "and burden light because of it.
I love you so, that should I love one whit
More than I do, mine heart would cease to beat.
As liquids when they have attain'd the heat
Of boiling do the chemist's skill outwit
To make them hotter—sooner apt to quit
Liquidity—even so do I, replete
With loving you, defy the power of art
To drop one lovedrop more into mine heart
Till Heaven have deepen'd its capacity.
I love you so, that if I could not be
Myself so loving—all the world above,
I would be you, inspiring such a love."

"CAN TIME, THOU ASK'ST, MY HEART FROM THINE ESTRANGE?"

" CAN time, thou ask'st, my heart from thine
      estrange ? "
She sang, " Beloved, love thou dost but mock !
Can hearts that love find time in time to change?—
That one tick of the great celestial clock
The angels hear, wherein we can but clasp
The thing we love and lay it on the tomb—

That fleeting breath, wherein we can but grasp
The keys of Heaven, when lo ! the gates uploom
And we stand trembling on the outer side.
Ask, rather, can a breeze fan out the sun ?
Love is eternal.   Heaven is its throne,
Infinitude its limit, God its guide.
And time can only teach to thee and me
A golden prelude to a love to be.''

"EARTH HATH MOMENTS."

" Beloved, earth hath moments when we need
    No proofs of Heav'n,'' she sang—''rare drops
      of time
That fall like elixir from celestial clime
Into the inner consciousness and spread
A sense of Eden thro' the wearied head.
Our spirits pulse ! spurn their material slime,
And leap, enfranchised, to a height sublime
To which nor science nor ritual nor creed
Had ever builded.   Thus, this golden trice,
When thou dost let the heaven of thine eyes
Drop on my stricken brows—now dews of pity,
Now beams of love, now cataracts of kisses—
Ah, love ! one leaps, in such an hour as this is,
The jasper walls of the Celestial City.

"THE PENDULUM MUST HAVE THE BACK-WARD SWING."

The pendulum must have the backward swing :
    Thus at what time I saw her raptur'd soul
Drawn to'ards beatitude's extremest pole,

I knew, ere long some secret inner spring
Would snap and send it earthward fluttering.
Thus swing our pendulum lives, 'twixt joy and dole,
'Twixt Heav'n and earth, until the twelfth-hour toll
Our destiny and loose our shackled wing
To go the way that hath no backward course.
Sweet Spirit of Temperance! steady thou our
    dreams—
Poise thou our wing mid-heav'n, teach us to miss
Both quicksand peak of joy and slough of remorse.
Yet, Youth, we thank thee for these keen extremes
That fit us better for the eternal choice.

"SOME DAY."

"SOME DAY—some day"—She had a gentle way
    Of singing that, that made it sound so sad
And far, far off.   "Some day we shall be glad
Again, Beloved, and our tardy May
Will bring the redder roses for the gray
And cheerless winter that so long has had
Its roots deep-buried in its snowy bed.
Mine own! we shall be happy yet—some day.
God will forgive us if we love too much,
Or gently chasten us with Gilead touch—
He knoweth that we love thro' Him alone—
Then ever and aye let us be true, mine own!
Here or beyond the stars, I may not say,
We shall be happy yet, some day—some day."

THALIA AND TERPSICHORE.

ALAS! soft spell of Eros—hearken there!
  A sudden rustling in the myrtle trees,
A merry laughter ringing on the breeze—
Terpsichore and Thalia, blooming pair!
One might have known ye twain were hiding here,
With flageolet and mask, sweet love to tease.
Yet stay, bright goddesses! Your spirits please
Me well. We poets and lovers cannot spare
Your merry intermeddling with our moods,
Lest we should reach more wide, or soar more high,
Or dive more deep, than wisdom's reed can measure.
My hand, idyllic Thalia! which includes
The lighter half my heart, lent cheerfully.
My foot, Terpsichore?—Mon metre, avec plaisir!

"WERE I A ROSE-VINE IN HER GARDEN GROWING."

(To Music.)

WERE I a rose-vine in her garden growing,
  Blowing, I'd grow so high, I'd blow so white,
So high and white I'd grow and blow, at night,
She'd think 'twas day, and when the wind was blow-
  ing
My petals thither and yon, she'd think 'twas snowing—
So thick, so quick, they'd dance and glance, so light,
So bright. And when with all its dainty might
Her tiny trowel o'er my roots came plowing,
By kind degrees I'd loose my earth-grip tight—
So subtly she would think 'twas all her doing!

But when old Winter came with frost and blight,
I'd turn on him a countenance unknowing—
Yea, scorn him, thorn him, till he took his flight-
Were I a rose-vine in her garden growing.

A VIRGINIA MOONSET.

SCENE : Lovely Orange-on-the-Rapidan ;
    At Peliso, headquarters once of Lee,
That only perfect man in history.
Time : Moonset. *Cast*—nay! that would mar the
    scene.
Some landskips need no *personæ*, I ween,
To give them sympathy, whatever be
The opinions of the schools.   Ideality
Could only hold the mirror here : in vain
Were any added touch of fancy's brush.
Pale, tottering Lady Moon ! thy waning charms
Were ever most alluring.   A deep hush
Is over all.   Almost I hear her steps.
Now—alas ! my *personæ*—in his brave arms
The Blue Ridge folds her, softly—and she sleeps.

"MAY'ST PEEL ME A PEACH?"

MAY'ST peel me a peach ? Aye me ! had Byron seen
    Thee at table, Lady, he had never made
That uncouth speech of his on breaking bread
With women : rather than out of love, I ween
He had fallen more in love with thee, thou queen
Of hostesses !—whose snowy board doth spread
Such dainty, dainty viands as might be fed

To Euterpe, seated on the Pierian green—
Can I, her humble harpbearer, resist
So delicate homage, from a hand so chaste,
A board so hospitable? An' thou insist,
Aye! peel me a peach, but peel it not in haste.
Beseech thee! not so nigh—but let me reach,
Lest I mistake the fingers for the peach!

MAM AGGY.—I.

WITH snowy-white bandanna, knotted neat
    About her head, and one pinn'd round her neck,
Tri-corner'd, o'er her dazzling homespun check,
I see her on the kitchen door-sill seat
Her faithful down, the golden yelks to beat
For Sunday's pound-cake—'round and 'round so
    quick
A fluttermill had envied her the trick!
What time with straws I might manipulate
The frothing whites—which, spill'd upon the ground,
I now bewail. She puts her black arms 'round
Me soothingly—no chiding word is spoken—
And sings, "*Dah-den!*"—seeing that my heart is
    broken—
"*Dah-den, dah-den*"—till I rock off to sleep.
The cake?—O never mind that. Eggs are cheap.

MAM AGGY.—II.

SHE had but one tooth to her homely name,
    And that but strong enough to munch a jumble,
Or meatskins, crispt till they fell all a-crumble—
Or *very* mellow pears. I liked the same.

So sometimes she need dodge me, poor old Mam !
But ah ! when on the green I had a tumble,
And lay there very still and white and humble,
How like a ministering angel then she came !
And lifted me, and sang that fond refrain
That always carried healing on its wings.
And to this day when in its venturings
My spirit gets a tumble on life's green,
From memory's phonograph there comes again
That Gilead lullaby—" *Dah-den, Dah-den.*"

THE MINUET.

IN powder'd periwig, and ruffled shirt,
   And proud knee-breeches with resplendent girth,
Our pious *grandpére* led our *grandemére* forth,
In bounteous mutton legs and swelling skirt,
In stately minuet to take a part,
Ye olden days, or ere the giddy earth
A-jigging went, alack !—No time for mirth,
No time for frivolous twirling heart to heart,
To lightsome roundelay—no time for fun ;
But time for grave consideration,
Time for deliberating means and ways,
For exercising heaven-bestowèd talents—
A coupee—and a long step—and a balance.
They danc'd in sonnets in ye olden days.

THE HEAVENLY MUSE.

AS out this vale I merg'd, a fulgent light
 Burst o'er my vision, blinding me with bliss—
An effluence supernal.   Certes 'tis
The beam that quenchèd Chaos and Old Night,
In the beginning, and did put to flight
The Stygian desolation.   Thus, I wis,
Blinded by beatific dizziness,
That ancient shepherd stood, when Oreb's height
Blaz'd forth God's secret.   From no oracle
Aonian could such luminous essence stream ;
'Tis Sinai's mount, or Zion's holy hill,
In gradual outline, with white wings a-gleam,
And dove-like brooding o'er Siloa's strand,
The Heavenlv Muse extendeth me a hand.

INVOCATION.

O THOU who leanest forth in splendor calm,
 Amidst the golden whirl of chiming spheres,
To catch the soft fall of Thy children's tears,
And pour out universes from Thy palm ;
Teach me from out my soul to lift a psalm
Not all-unmeet for omnisentient ears,
Which thro' the distance hear the mellowing years

Glide down the stalk of Time, like drops of balm—
Which heard the Future even before the Past,—
Touch Thou my spirit in its protean youth
To nobler issues, so that when above
Thy summons call me, I shall have amast
Something to lay upon the fane of Truth,
Something to offer at the shrine of Love.

MIZPAH.

A CALYX of dead rose-leaves.   I know not
  If Mareschal Niel, or Nonpareil, or Tea,
La France, or Cloth of Gold, or Cherokee,
Countess of Folkstone, or Marie Van Hout,
Or Rainbow—time hath wiped the colors out.
I only know a lov'd one gave it me,
And 'twixt two sacred leaves I reverently
Laid it, to mark a well-belovèd spot
In Genesis.   Beneath the golden skies
Of southern California there is
A giant pepper-tree, whose utmost bark,
To its limbs' ends, is o'er-fleck'd with La Marque
Roses.   For this magnificent bouquet
Would I exchange these faded rose-leaves ?   Nay.

GOD FIRST.

" GOD *first, and then we cannot love too well.*"
    So be it, Dearest, betwixt thee and me.
God first, and last, and all, and let us be
Dear to each other only as we dwell
In Him, and He in us.   Emanuel,
" God with us," be our passport-word ; which we

May well link out with kisses, joyously ;
Or chime to laughter, like a silver bell ;
Or music out in sonnet or in song ;
Or balm with tears of tender sacrifice ;
Or pass in silent sympathy along
The happy level of our trustful eyes ;
Or waft in prayer-waves to that far sweet home,
Where Christ will keep the echo till we come.

GRACE.

THAT which sufficient for us is ; whereby
    Our strength in weakness may be perfected.
That which from Heaven is like sunshine shed,
Alike upon the lowly and the high—
Which even the poorest may most richly enjoy—
Withheld but from the proud.   What to a blade
Of summer grass, that hangs a dying head,
A drop of evening dew is, gradually
Seeping into its roots ; that unto faith,
Tried in the furnace, is a drop of grace
Shed from the Mercy Seat.   What to the path
Of the lost pilgrim in the wilderness
The Evening Star is, that is grace to doubt.
That which what life were blameless, being without ?

"WE MAKE MISTAKES, AND GOD O'ER-RULETH THEM."

" *WE make mistakes, and God o'erruleth them,*"
    To me, once sitting at her feet, she said.
I took the crystal thought, all unafraid,
And held it where God's pure sunlight could stream

Thro' it full into my heart; and, in this beam,
The past was simplified and hallowèd.
Doubt-mists shone rainbows; mysteries outspread
Transparent wings; blocks that did barriers seem
Prov'd pavingstones, or curbstones, for the strait
And narrow way that leads to Heaven's gate;
Briers were rosebuds; wither'd leaves, rich soil;
Sorrows were sacred backgrounds, joys to foil.
So in faith's crown I set as central gem—
" *We make mistakes, and God o'erruleth them.*"

BEATITUDE THE SECOND.

HER life, she said, a blessed one had been.
     Then whyfore, was my wonder, is her face
So sorrow-chasten'd?   Now full well I trace
Beatitude the second in her mien,—
A dying-daily unto self, I ween,
A pressing onward in the sacred race,
Sandal'd with faith and panoplied with grace;
A heartache there I read, grown to a serene
Patience, thro' easing aches of others' hearts,
And thro' prayer-service.   Aye, a blessed life,
And clear to read.   As daughter, sister, wife,
Mother, and friend, she has climb'd the Christian stair,
To where reflected Heaven-light imparts
A peace that makes her widow'd face a prayer.

IDA ASH.

HOW did she come to me ?—or was it I
   Who came to her?—or did we come together
Of one accord? I know nor whence nor whither
We twain were journeying—was it yesterday,
Or some dim preëxistence?—Destiny,
With iron tread—or Chance, blown like a feather—
Or clash of wandering stars—or freak of weather,
That brought our hands to clasp in sympathy,
Our eyes to meet in music, and our souls
To leap en rapport?—Nay! as well divine
Which of two intermelting dewdrops rolls
First into the other. Whyfore seek a sign?
I only know, 'twas night : a voice : a flash
Of nereid eyes—then day—and Ida Ash.

PARABLES.

THE SOWER.

BEHOLD, a sower goeth forth to sow.
    Some seed fall by the wayside, and are there
Of fowls devour'd. Some where the earth is rare
And stony fall, upspring, but are laid low,
Being rootless, by the morrow's sun. Some blow
Their careless way amidst the thorn and brier, ,
Flourish a day, then seized and chokèd are.
But other some in good ground fall, and grow.
Thus at Gennesaret, beside the sea,
What time the multitudes were gather'd round,
First parabled the great Sower—even He
Whose every word-seed, rooted in good ground,
An hundredfold to-day is bringing forth
Of joy and peace in all the ends of earth.

THE WHEAT AND THE TARES.

A SECOND parable put He forth and said,
    Again heaven's kingdom may be liken'd to
A man who with good seeds his field did sow,
But whilst his servants slept there enterèd
The enemy sowing tares, that where the blade
Of wheat upsprung, upsprung the tare-blade too.
The servant of the householder would go

To uproot them, but his master him forbade,
Saying, Nay, lest peradventure unawares
Thou uproot the wheat-blade likewise. Side by side
Till harvest time together let them bide ;
Then say to the reapers, Gather first the tares,
Bundle and bind and burn them ; then the wheat
Into my storehouse garner, clean and sweet.

THE MUSTARD SEED, THE LEAVEN, AND THE GOODLY PEARL.

AGAIN unto a grain of mustard seed
  Our poet Saviour similizes heaven
Establishing its throne on earth,—which, even
Tho' smallest of all seeds it be indeed,
Grows yet to an herb the branches whereof spread
So tree-like that therein is lodgment given
To birds of the air. Again, like unto leaven
God's kingdom is, the which a woman hid
In meal three measuresful, till lo, the whole
Betimes was leaven'd. Now, like a great-pric'd gem,
Which when the merchant saw he straightway sold
All that he had and bought it. Thus parable
On parable at Gennesaret He told,
And without parable spake He not to them.

THE TEN TALENTS.

ON Olive's mount this metaphor He drew:
  As a man journeying to a distant land,
So is God's kingdom,—who did first command
His stewards 'round him, that his revenue

Be husbanded.   Five talents one, another two,
Another one, he gave, to wisely spend.
He with the five and he with the two did lend
Their treasure out to the exchangers, who
Reimburs'd it to them doubled ; so that when
Their lord return'd he said to them, Well done,
Ye good and faithful servants !   But alas
For him who hid his talent, having but one ;
Which when his master heard, his edict was,
Take it from him and give to the one with ten.

THE TEN VIRGINS.

WENT forth with lamps ten virgins once to meet
     The bridegroom.   Five were wise, and they did
          bare
Oil in their vessels, and five foolish were,
And they no oil took with them.   Whilst that yet
The bridegroom tarried, all in slumber sweet
O'erpass'd the hours, till on the midnight air
There came a cry, The bridegroom doth appear !
Then forthwith got the virgins to their feet.
Pray give us of your oil, the foolish plead,
Our empty lamps to fill.   But made reply
The wise, Not so, but go ye forth and buy.
What time they went, the wise were welcom'd in
The chamber by the bridegroom.   Later when
The foolish knockt, I know you not, he said.

THE GOOD SAMARITAN.

ONE ask'd, Who is my neighbor? Jesus said :
    A certain man going from Jerusalem
Fell among thieves, who stript and wounded him,
And then departed, leaving him half dead.
By chance that way a certain priest estray'd,
But when the wounded would his pity claim,
He pass'd by on the other side.   The same
A certain Levite did, which saw and fled.
But now a good Samaritan pass'd near,
And seeing him took pity, and did pour
Oil in his wounds, and to an inn did bear
Him swift, and left him there, provided for.
Which now was neighbor unto him that fell?
He that compassion had.   Thou answerest well.

THE LOST SHEEP.

MURMUR'D a Pharisee, Lo, publican
    Receiveth He, and doth with sinner dine.
Then allegorically did He define
His purpose therein, saying, Now what man,
Having an hundred sheep, is there, who, when
He lose one, doth not leave the ninety-and-nine,
Back to the fold his wandering sheep to win?—
Which having found, rejoicingly then
Bearing it home, he saith to his neighbors, Lo,
That which was lost is found ; rejoice with me.
In the presence of the angels, even so
O'er one returning sinner is more bliss
Than over ninety-and-nine just persons is,
Which have not gone astray.   Thus answer'd He.

THE UNMERCIFUL SERVANT.

THIS lesson taught He at Capernaum :
    Once of his servants all a certain king
Did take account, and on discovering
One was his debtor to a goodly sum,
Which he had not to pay, he bade him come
Before him to be bound.   But he did fling
Him prostrate down with such a piteous spring
Of tears, the king relax'd, unfix'd his doom,
And gave him time of grace.   As out he past,
A fellow-slave he met which was his debtor,
Whom, when he pray'd for grace, he bound in fetter.
The king now, waxen wroth, the ingrate cast
To the tormentors, till he pay his dues.
Likewise the unforgiving God will use.

THE RICH FOOL.

A CERTAIN rich man's ground brought forth much
    grain.
Within himself he thought, What shall I do?—
Seeing that he had no place where to bestow
His fruits.   This shall I do, he thought again—
Pull down my barns and greater build ; which when
I have done, unto my soul I shall say, Lo,
My soul, look thou about thee and see how
Much goods for many years thou hast uplain ;
Eat, drink, and take thine ease, and merry be.
But came God's voice from Heaven, saying, Thou
    fool,
This night shall be requir'd of thee thy soul.

Whose then shall be this bounty thou dost hoard?
Who layeth up treasure on earth, even so is he,
Not being rich toward God.   Thus taught our Lord.

THE FIG-TREE AND ALL THE TREES.

LOVE shall wax cold, and friends offence shall take,
 Break faith, and part, and hate with rancorous
   passion;
New Christs arise, with such smooth revelation
The faith of all but the elect 'twill shake;
Earth, slinking to some pestilent hole, shall quake—
The sun a shroud spread o'er her tribulation.
In those days shall be that abomination
Of desolation whereof Daniel spake.
Then shall God's angels come with bugles down,
And gather in, from heav'n's four winds, His own.
Behold the fig-tree now, and all the trees.
When they bud forth then know ye is summer nigh,
So when these signs abound know ye thereby
Appeareth suddenly the Prince of Peace.

AT TRUTH'S DOOR.

KNOCK, and it shall be open'd unto thee;
 Not once and softly, but again and yet
Again, even until honest sweat-beads set
Thy brow with labor's gems—reiterately
Knock without ceasing, midnight, dawn and day,
Thro' numbing winter and thro' summer heat—
And, ah! thro' all the low south's breathing sweet
Alluring spices in the opposing way.

The deeper be the silence therewithin,
The louder, steadier be thy summoning.
And if it chance, as thou dost breathless lean
Against the door, thou hear some little thing
Creak at thine ardor—faint not, neither cringe :
'Tis envy percht upon the yielding hinge.

FAITH AND SUPERSTITION.

TWO blind men thro' death's valley-shadows dense
Once I saw journeying.   By two asses one
Was led : his name was Superstition ;
The asses were Hearsay and Ignorance—
With many an awkward balk and freakish prance
Now dragging jerkily, now on the run,
They led him helter-skelter, while the sun
Sunk surely o'er the hill-tops.   At one glance
I observ'd the other kept an even path
Unerring toward the light, tho' likewise blind.
Approaching him, in reverence, from behind,
I ask'd why this great difference?   He said,
Tho' blind, I feel the light—my name is Faith.
He cannot feel, so thuswise needs be led.

ABRAHAM.

CLAY that did lack a flaw—the potter's choice
　　To mould a vessel for His special grace—
Obedient Abram! with thy heaven-turned face,
And ear uplifted for the guiding Voice.
What wonder, when the message from the skies
Came suddenly down, thou wast found in thy place,
Ready to sign the covenant and to embrace
The heavenly adoption; ready to rise
Out of thy "Abram"-hood, thy "fatherhood,"
To "Abraham," "father of a multitude?"
As in unquestioning obedience bow'd
Thou standest there, to doubting Thomases
How art thou a divine antithesis,
Thou "Father of the Faithful"—"Friend of God."

JACOB.

THAT champion wrestler of the spiritual world,
　　Jacob!—who fac'd the Almighty at Peniel
In battle, nor would let Him go until
He brought the blessing down—thrice earthward
　　hurl'd,
Upspringing thrice again—he sway'd—he swirl'd—
Nightlong he wrestled, till at last he fell,
Thigh-pierced, disjointed—but victorious still!

No longer now a zealous dreamer, curl'd
At foot of heavenly ladder, whereupon
Angels ascending and descending run
God's errands whilst He slept ; no longer call'd
Jacob, "supplanter," but a king, install'd
With heavenly insignia and diadem,
Israel, "soldier of God"—root of the Lamb.

JOSEPH.

THOU rainbow Joseph ! How the feminine eye,
    Down-diving thro' antiquity's abysses,
Delighteth in thy pearl—ah ! surely this is
A pearl of goodly price, man's chastity—
A jewel to carry with him to the sky.
As modesty a woman's chiefest grace is,
So chastity a man's.   In ancient places
We find no rarer type than thine (we sigh
Amidst our admiration, since so rare)
And wear thee in our heart because of it,
Chiefly.   Though we would not withal forget
Thine other Christ-like charm, almost as sweet—
Thy spirit of forgiveness.   If my prayer
Were for one double portion, 'twere of that.

MOSES.

THOU who conceiv'dest the beginning of things,
    Who broughtest God's creation to the front,
And borest with thy staff and rod the brunt
Of genesis warfare—without horse or wings—
Monarch foot-soldier, ancient King of kings !—

Who parley'd'st with the Almighty on the mount ;
And smotest granite into crystal fount ;
Braving the darkness, famine, plagues, and stings
Of the Egyptian exodus ; who did'st toil
Thro' genealogic numberings ; and compile
The law Levitical, with nicest care ;
And recapitulate, laboriously,
A tedious length of deuteronomy—
At last to glimpse sweet Canaan from afar.

JOB.

UPLOOMING in peculiar majesty,
 The epic hero of the ancient Word—
Martyr of Uz !—Let other harps be stirr'd
To pæan thy patience—thine independence be
My extolling theme. Now, like some giant tree,
Storm-tost, yet root-unshaken, with no bird
To cheer thy branches, but a few absurd
Crows cawing there a hollow mockery
Of consolation—which thou dost outspew
As did the mouth divine the Laodicean
Lukewarmness. Prostrate now, with pain a-squirm,
But to thy conscious uprightness still true,
Lifting to Him who slayeth a trustful pæan,
And scorning human criticism, tho' a worm.

ISAIAH.

CLARION of Christ, herald of Calvary—
 Isaiah ! "the gospel prophet "—without peer
Save only one, the Apocalyptic seer—
How was Jerusalem's idolatry

O'er-rioting her ancient dignity,
When thou did'st startle the Judean ear
With thine alarum-trumpet, bold and clear!
Alas! and how thy woeful prophecy
True cameth quickly! Lo, Jerusalem
The Beautiful, where crumbleth now thy fame?
But, ah! how comfortably did'st thou forecast
For them who mourn in Zion: the Beulah-feast,
The nuptials of the Church with the I AM—
The marriage-supper of the Bride and Lamb!

CHRIST.

DAY-SPRING, Deliverer, Just and Holy One,
　　The Way, the Faithful Witness, Prince of Peace,
The Bread of God, Lord of our Righteousness,
Our Passover, true Vine, and Corner-stone,
Adam the Second, only begotten Son,
Image of God, desire of every race,
Our Counselor, our Advocate for grace,
The Morning Star, Horn of Salvation,
Root and offspring of David, Israel's Lamb,
Shepherd of souls, Emanuel, the I AM,
The First and Last, Salvation's only Name,
Our yesterday—to-day—for aye the same,
Light of the world, and Conqueror of death,
Author and Finisher of our Faith.

JESUS.

CHRIST-dazzled eyes we turn how comfortably
   To Thee, O gentle Friend, sweet Nazarene !
John-like upon thy bosom fain to lean.
O eyes we love to look in ! eyes that see
Beneath our faults our human frailty—
Forgiving eyes ! and hands so strong and clean
We love to feel our frail hands nestling in ;
We kiss the white scars where thine agony
Once flow'd for us, the stripes that heal'd our pain
And paid the price of our infirmities,
And in our blissful gratitude are fain
To separate even Judas from his kiss,
And, if we have them, say to our enemies,
"To-morrow meet with me in Paradise."

JOHN.

WHY do we love thee most, beloved John ?
   For that on Jesus' bosom thou did'st lean—
"Whom Jesus lov'd "—no sweeter seal, I ween,
Of honor ever yet was set upon
A human brow—*whom Jesus lov'd*—the one
Pure lover that the world hath ever known,
The one pure bosom that hath ever been
For human tenderness a blissful throne—
All others but approximately tend
To purity.   Aye, even as a friend
Embosometh a friend, did Jesus pin
John in his breast, a redolent heart-blossom.
Ah ! I do love to think that Jesus e'en
Did have a pet : John lean'd upon His bosom.

PETER.

"HENCEFORTH a rock." What time the Patmos bliss
  We wing with John, 'tis safe to feel that thou,
Peter, art our foundation-stone below,
When earthward back we reel. What grace was this—
" *Henceforth a rock* "—no longer to Christ's voice
A hearkener, a " Simon," but even now
A piece of that firm grantite whence did flow
The Horeb miracle—that rock which is
" Higher than I," yet deeper than very hell—
And yet, alas, how brief a time until
Thou did'st become a great rock of offense,
A mount of salt, a river of penitence ;
But soon recrystalliz'd, more firm and better.
With Luther we "thank God for Simon Peter !"

PAUL.

PAUL—giant of didactic geniuses !
  Who, God-informèd, dost of God inform.
Where doth thy swift-revolving ardor charm
Us most?—Where thou dost zealously impress
Upon the Roman mind God's righteousness ;
Or liftest the Corinthian alarm ;
Or layest bare thy lacerated arm
In argument with Thessalonian Greece ;
Or in Philippian acknowledgment
Minglest with gratitude thy discontent
Divine, at man's ingratitude and doubt?
In every phase we find thee masterful,
But at Damascus thou'rt most admirable,
Where thou the courage had'st to face about.

ISCARIOT.

A RARE kaleidoscope one day I found—
  Logostos' gift to man.   With olive tree
'Twas fram'd, and Shittim wood of Araby;
In Babylonian leather was it bound,
And with pure gold of Ophir rimm'd around.
With reverent hand I turn'd it charmèdly:
Twelve crystal fragments of divinity,
Combining 'round one central diamond:
Chrysolite, sardonyx, jasper and sardius,
Jacinth, chrysoprasus, beryl and emerald,
Topaz, chalcedone, sapphire and amethyst—
The apostolic twelve—all luminous,
Save flaw'd Iscariot, a beryl cold,
Refracting e'en the rays of diamond Christ.

EVE.

OR ere into their bower of innocence
  The guileful serpent-fiend had glittering stalkt,
And smooth into her charmèd ear had talkt
That honeyed and perditious confidence
For which our earthly woe is recompense—
Which earth's prime Paradisian purpose balkt;
Whiles yet down Eden-aisles they blissful walkt,
Or ere deflower'd by disobedience—
Is our most sweet First Mother sweetest here?
Nay! for since when in the heav'ns God hung His bow
Beauty but comes to us thro' prism-ray
Of tear-mists.   Even so Eve is sweetest where
"They hand in hand with wandering steps and slow
Thro' Eden took their solitary way."

CAIN'S WIFE.

EASTWARD from Eden in the land of Nod,
    Cain found a maiden in a mist. Whence sprung,
Who knoweth? Of what lineage? Of what tongue?
Whyfore her wandering? and whither her road?—
Mysteries unsearchable by word of God,
Which curtaining silence therearound hath hung.
And yet 'tis meet this maid be not unsung
Of psalmist, and to her be not unshow'd
Some gentle deference; for the saints owe much
To one who was foremother " of all such
As handle harp and organ."   Hence I am fain
To brush from strings of mine this pæan-strain
To Jubal's ancestress—nay, to resist
Thy claim is past my power, sweet maid o' the mist.

HAGAR.

BËER-LAHÄI-ROI, the well between
    Kedesh and Bedad in Shur's wilderness,
Where banisht Hagar in midnight distress
Is found of the angel, weeping—'tis the scene
Where stand with claspt hands Pathos and Chagrin
And interchange their subtlest sympathies,
Saddest and bitterest of heart-histories,—
In musing down the storied past terrene.
Of the seed-royal visited, innocently,
Too sudden lifted from hand-maidenhood,
What wonder danc'd with pride the Egyptian blood,
And barren Sarai should despisèd be—
She banisht? Now, this angel-promised child—
Ishmael—what solace! "a wandering man and wild."

SARAH.

IN the tent-door in Mamre's plains she sat,
  Old and in years well-stricken, whiles her lord
Beneath the hospitable tree outpour'd
The fragrant milk, and serv'd the tender meat
Unto the angel guests, and they did eat,
What time she, modest, listen'd, nor once stirr'd
The tent-door from behind. What wondrous word
Now wooes her ear and makes her heart to beat
A laughing lilt? Sooth, shall she, waxen old,
Of God be visited, as is now foretold
Of heavenly presence? Comes a son soon after—
Isaac (which, being interpreted, is " laughter ")—
"The father of twelve princes." Now she sleeps,
Blest, in Machpelah's cave. And Abraham weeps.

REBEKAH.

THREE pictures of Rebekah are stain'd upon
  The temple-panes of sacred reminiscence.
One where with bubbling pitcher tipt she hastens
To quench the stranger's thirst—familiar one.
Now, meeting Isaac where he stands alone
Beneath the meditating stars, she fastens
Her modest vail about her, with sweet prescience
Of being woo'd. Here, on her favorite son,
With fingers deft and most exquisite tact,
She sews the treacherous kid-skins to deceive
A blind deathbed and Esau to deprive,
That weakling, of the blessing coveted.
Alas the guile ! Yet, rue it as we need,
This charms us too. 'Twas such a mother's act.

14

RACHEL.

RACHEL, the damsel, leadeth Laban's sheep
To well of Haran, from whose mouth away
Jacob the stone swift rolleth, and—sweet day!—
Kisseth her, lifteth his voice up, and doth weep.
Rachel, the wife, high-mounted on the steep
Of camel's back, with nicest policy,
O'er Laban's household-gods her skirts doth lay,
The stolen treasure from his search to keep.
Rachel, the mother, with prescient despair,
Lifteth a wail and bitter lamentation,
Which pierceth e'en to Jeremiah's ear,
And is fulfilled in Herod's devastation.
For Bethlehem's unborn firstborn weepeth she,
Slain at the suck—nor comforted will be.

RUTH AND NAOMI.

"WHERE hast thou glean'd to-day?" What
sweeter twain
Of Bible women than Naomi and Ruth?—
One thrice-bereavèd and a widow in truth—
"Mara"—her blind eyes pouring bitter rain—
Husbandless, sonless, desolated—fain
To flee the happy meadows of her youth,
Now barren of delight, and black with drought,
For Bethlehem in Judah, there to glean
Ephah of meagre barley.—"Nay, intreat
Me not from following after thee—
Where diest thou I die, there buried be."
When prone at Boaz' amiable feet,
What lifts the sweet Moabitess above
Her sex? That rarest passion, friendship-love.

VASHTI.

A HASUERUS maketh royal feast.
    From Ethiope's border and from India's shore
They troop, for days an hundred and fourscore,
To Shushan's hall—a glittering throng—to test
His sumptuous bounty, and the night to waste
In purple revelry. "Whiles yet we pour
The golden vintage down, bring ye before
My majesty the Queen," is his behest,
"That in her beauteous charms the eyes may lave
Of these my merry guests." "But Queen Vashti
Refus'd to come," 'tis said. O charming sound!
Fine spirit-flash thro' woman history!
"Vashti the Beautiful"—aye, and Vashti·the brave—
Who to be modest durst to be discrown'd.

DORCAS.

" F ULL of good works and almsdeeds which she did."
    What nobler epitaph on tomb to grave
Than this brief character the Apostle gave
Dorcas of Joppa? 'Round the sorrowing bed
(Where Peter swiftly had been summonèd)
We see the weeping widows stand and wave
The goodly coats and garments that the brave
Deft fingers of dame Tabitha had made—
Mayhap in midnight watches—till, alas,
(How simply sad the words) "it came to pass
That she was sick and died." But "Tabitha, arise,"
Saith Peter now; and, as she opes her eyes,
He lifts her whole. So in sweet Beulah Land
May Christ take all dead workers by the hand.

MIRIAM, DEBORAH AND ANNA.

SWEET o'er the centuried tumult rise the calm
    Inspired voices of three women seers,
The sacred poetesses, without peers
In Israel. First, timbrel'd Miriam,
Leading her sisters, with victorious psalm,
Past the Red Sea into the heart of Shur's
Brine-flowing wilderness. Next, she who wears
The ermine—Deborah, singing 'neath her palm,
"The mountains melted before Israel's host."
Last, widow'd Anna—and beloved most—
True to one husband more than threescore years,
Serving the Lord with fastings, psalms and prayers
Both day and night. First after Simeon
To lift an anthem over Mary's Son.

MAGDALENE.

"WOMAN, why weepest thou?" "For that my Lord
    Away they have taken, and I know not where
Him they have laid." And is this woman, fair
And tender, she from whom the entering Word
Had late out-cast seven devils?—and now stirr'd
By such sweet desolation for her dear
Lost Master. Is this the same that bare
The precious alabaster box and pour'd
The ointment on His head, and washt His feet
With tears, and wiped them with her locks of hair?—
Whose sins, tho' many, yet were first forgiven,
"For she loved much"—O judgment pure from
    Heaven!
" Last at the cross, first at the sepulchre "—
And first our risen Lord went forth to meet.

MARY.

ALL gentle influences now descend,
    From whatsoever sources pure and high,
And hover o'er my reverent harp whiles I
Sing of the Mother of that Heavenly Friend
Before whom every knee at last must bend
And every head low bow.   Sweet mystery !—
Virgin conceiver of Emmanuel by
The Holy Spirit.   Name most reverend
Of womankind.   The pearl of goodliest price
Washt by the waves of time from Heaven's shore
To shores terrene.   Last, sweetest blossom shed
By that frail flower, humility, ere its eyes
It clos'd to ope this side of Heaven no more.
Mary, Mother of Jesus—all is said.

IN THE CRUCIBLE.

I WATCH'D the jeweler fix his sensitive eye
    Over the crucible, turn on the test
Of fire—now gaze with nice-pois'd interest
Into the bubbling ore.   No passer-by
Dare near him, nor with pestering questions ply
That awful monarchy of stillness, lest
The sovereign sense be jarr'd.   With swift arrest
He turns the white heat off, for instantly
His face is mirror'd—'tis done !
                Even so, I thought,
Hath God through fires of affliction brought
His chosen ones, to where they imag'd back

His features—when His hand was swift to slack
The testing-fires.   Then came into my mind
One face, pain-purified and thrice-refined.

"IN THOUGHT THE SEVEN GREAT MOUNTS
I VISITED."

IN thought the seven great mounts I visited
   That sentinel the sacred centuries :
First, *Ararat*, the ark's calm resting-place ;
Next, that dear Mizpah-heap where Laban made
The covenant with Jacob—*Gilead ;*
Law-giving *Horeb*, then, whereon God's face
Shone in the bush, and where the still small voice
Came to Elijah ; *Sinai*, whence were read
The ten commandments ; *Zion's* brow serene,
Where rose the temple ; *Pisgah*, from whose height
Canaan was glimps'd of Moses, ere he slept ;
And—grandest, saddest—the Ascension scene,
Sweet *Olivet*, where David made his flight
From Absalom his son—where Jesus wept.

"THERE ARE TEN PRECIOUS STREAMS I
LOVE TO TRACE."

THERE are ten precious streams I love to trace
   Thro' sacred soil : *Hiddekel, Euphrates,*
Pison, and *Gihon,* bounding Paradise ;
Jabbok, the conquering Jacob's wrestling-place ;
Arnon, where, merging out the wilderness,
Moses triumphant landed 'neath clear skies ;

The brook of *Cherith*, where, led of God's voice,
Elijah hid and was for many days
Fed of the ravens; *Kishon*, where the brave
Deborah rais'd her matchless song of praise
At Sisera's defeat—death-pool of Baal.
Kedron, of Christ cross'd, after the betrayal;
And—noblest, dearest—*Jordan's* blessed wave,
Our Saviour suffer'd to o'ersweep His face.

A PSALM OF COMFORT.

MOURNERS in Zion, your mourning is not vain.
Comfort ye! God is powerful, God is kind:
His promise is, the broken heart to bind,
The feeble knees to strengthen and sustain.
If at Bethesda's pool ye wait, in pain—
If others press before and entrance find
To the angel-troubled waters, whilst ye, blind
And tottering, on the outside needs remain—
Look up! One there a place prepareth us
Within His father's many-mansion'd house.
If at Gate Beautiful, he will hear your moans,
And send you leaping o'er the temple-stones;
Or if in Jordan's wave ye strive, have faith!—
The everlasting arms are underneath.

NARCISSUS.

EMBLEM of vanity. Once a beautiful youth
Enamor'd of himself (so runs the myth),
Gaz'd on his image in a fount: forthwith
He chang'd into a white narcissus. Sooth,

A specious story 'tis,—thy face so smooth,
Thy breath so unctuous-sweet, thy stem so lithe,
Thy head so drooping, and thy smile so blithe ;
And yet I love thee better—as in truth
All things I better love—in thy divine
Significance than in thy mythic pose :
The "Rose of Sharon"—and Isaiah's " rose "—
The Church of Christ—that made the wilderness
To blossom, and the solitary place.
Emblem of holiness—flower of Nazarene.

ANEMONE.

SAD flower! of Flora banish'd from the fold,
    Jealous, since her beloved Zephyrus
Smil'd on thee, not ungracious—exil'd thus
To pine thy days upon the desert wold,
Unwoo'd, unwooable, unless Boreas bold
O'ertake thee, and in passion's impetus
Blow open thy chaste bosom, covetous
To snatch thy golden heart.   And yet, " Behold
The lilies of the field "—for such thou art—
Carpeting the holy plains of Palestine—
Gennesaret's glory, and outrivalling
Solomon's purple with thy crimson skirt,
For which thou toil'd'st not, neither did'st thou spin.
Glad flower! that kiss'd the feet of Israel's King.

L'ENVOI.

A VISION OF ART.

I.

DENSE midway up an awful mountain-steep,
  Two maidens meet, who have not met before.
Each journeys from a valley-land; each o'er
Her heart wears Art's insignia. One keeps
Her eye fix'd on a star; the other weeps,
O'erwearied, but preserves a none less sure
Upward advance, o'ercoming more and more
The beetling distance; till, in mercy, Sleep
O'ertakes them, meeting, and upon a bed
Of mossy ease, beside a lulling stream,
Enclasps them softly. Straightway now 'twould seem
They had reach'd the toil'd-for summit, but instead
Of being the topmost pinnacle, behold
Swift peak o'ercapping peak on view is roll'd.

II.

SOON waking, certes had these maidens twain
  Fainted of sheer despair, and backward bent
A baffled course, had not the each been sent
To uphold the other in this hour of pain.
Down the dread steep they gaze, then up again
To the o'erfrowning height. Shall they, half-spent
With half a pilgrimage, still upward strain

A laboring ascent, at last to find
Vast distances beyond, unreckonèd?
Bright underneath the inviting valleys spread
Their bowers of indolence; but brighter far
Beckons o'erhead the spirit-guiding star.
Now meet their crossing eyes—and up, where either
Alone had swoon'd, they lightly mount together.

MY SONNETS.

MY sonnets—how I love you! You have been
  My lighthouse-tower, wherein the lamp of Truth,
By sorrow hung, safe o'er the reefs of youth
Hath guided me to womanhood's serene,
Vine-shaded shores—my safety-ark, wherein,
Under Hope's iris archway, I have sail'd smooth
To Faith's calm Ararat. Loath and more loath
I grow to quit your dear confines, and lean
I more and yet more upon them for support;
Slow to meander forth on serious wing
Into those Daphne-dappled meads of Art,
A prey to vain conceits, or fancy's sport;
Rather content my sweets to be emptying
Into this classic mould for poet's heart.